"I think it would be better if we kept last night as a one-off. I don't want to have an affair with you...." Ella faltered, flushing when Vadim's piercing blue gaze settled thoughtfully on her face. She had the unnerving feeling that he could read the jumble of emotions whirling around in her head.

"Neither of us wants to be tied down in a relationship," she reminded him, despising herself for the way her heart rate quickened when he dropped onto the bed and wound a few strands of her hair around his fingers.

"I agree," he said coolly. "But surely the very fact that we have no desire for a relationship makes us ideal candidates for an affair? There's nothing to stop us being lovers. And besides," he murmured, his voice dropping to a deep, sensual tone that caressed her senses, "one night was not enough for either of us—was it, Ella?"

All about the author...
Chantelle Shaw

CHANTELLE SHAW lives on the Kent coast, five minutes from the sea, and does much of her thinking about the characters in her books while walking on the beach. An avid reader from an early age, she found that school friends used to hide their books when she visited, but Chantelle would retreat into her own world, and she still writes stories in her head all the time.

Chantelle has been blissfully married to her own tall, dark and very patient hero for more than twenty years and has six children. She began to read Harlequin® romances as a teenager, and throughout the years of being a stay-at-home mum to her brood, she found that romance fiction helped her to stay sane! Her aim is to write books that provide an element of escapism, fun and of course romance for the countless women who juggle work and a home life and who need their precious moments of "me" time. She enjoys reading and writing about strong-willed, feisty women and even stronger-willed sexy heroes.

Chantelle is at her happiest when writing. She is particularly inspired while cooking dinner, which unfortunately results in a lot of culinary disasters! She also loves gardening, taking her very badly behaved terrier for walks and eating chocolate (followed by more walking—at least the dog is slim!).

Chantelle Shaw

RUTHLESS RUSSIAN, LOST INNOCENCE

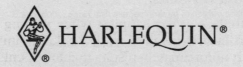

HARLEQUIN®

TORONTO • NEW YORK • LONDON
AMSTERDAM • PARIS • SYDNEY • HAMBURG
STOCKHOLM • ATHENS • TOKYO • MILAN • MADRID
PRAGUE • WARSAW • BUDAPEST • AUCKLAND

Recycling programs
for this product may
not exist in your area.

ISBN-13: 978-0-373-12920-1

RUTHLESS RUSSIAN, LOST INNOCENCE

First North American Publication 2010.

www.eHarlequin.com

Printed in U.S.A.

RUTHLESS RUSSIAN, LOST INNOCENCE

CHAPTER ONE

The Louvre Auditorium—Paris

IT HAPPENED in an instant. A fleeting glance across the crowded auditorium of the Louvre and *wham*, Ella felt as though she had been struck by a lightning bolt.

The man was standing some distance away, surrounded by a group of seriously chic Frenchwomen who were all vying for his attention. Her first impression in those few heart-stopping seconds when their eyes met was that he was tall, dark and devastatingly handsome—but when she tore her gaze from his piercing blue stare she instinctively added the word *dangerous* to the list.

Shaken by her reaction to a complete stranger, she stared down at her champagne glass, dismayed to find that her hands were trembling, and tried to concentrate on her conversation with a music journalist from the culture section of *Paris Match*.

'The audience were enraptured by you tonight, Mademoiselle Stafford. Your performance of Prokofiev's second violin concerto was truly outstanding.'

'Thank you.' Ella smiled faintly at the journalist, but she was still supremely conscious of the intense scrutiny of the man standing on the other side of the room, and it took all her willpower to resist turning her head. It was almost a relief when Marcus appeared at her side.

'You know everyone's saying a star has been born tonight?' he greeted her excitedly. 'You were bloody marvellous, Ella. I've just sneaked a preview of the review Stephen Hill is writing for *The Times,* and I quote—"Stafford's passion and technical bravura are out of this world. Her musical brilliance is dazzling, and her performance tonight cements her place as one of the world's top violinists." Not bad, eh?' Marcus could not hide his satisfaction. 'Come on—you need to circulate. There are at least half a dozen other journalists who want to interview you.'

'Actually, if you don't mind, I'd really like to go back to the hotel.'

Marcus's smile slipped when he realised that Ella was serious. 'But this is your big night,' he protested.

Ella bit her lip. 'I realise that the party is an ideal opportunity for more publicity, but I'm tired. The concert was draining.' Particularly when she'd spent the few hours before her solo performance ravaged by nerves, she thought ruefully. Music was her life, but the crippling stage fright she suffered every time she played in public was far from enjoyable, and sometimes she wondered if pursuing a career as a soloist was what she really wanted when it made her physically sick with fear.

'You attracted an A-list audience tonight, and you can't just disappear,' Marcus argued. 'I've seen at least two ministers from the French government, not to mention a Russian oligarch.' He glanced over Ella's shoulder and gave a low whistle. 'Don't look now, but Vadim Aleksandrov is heading this way.'

With a heavy sense of inevitability Ella turned her head a fraction, and felt her heart slam beneath her ribs when her eyes clashed once more with a startling blue gaze. The man was striding purposefully towards her, and she stared transfixed at the masculine beauty of his classically sculpted features and his jet-black hair swept back from his brow.

'Who is he?' she whispered to Marcus.

'A Russian billionaire—made his fortune in mobile phones and now owns a satellite television station, a British newspaper and a property empire that is said to include half of Chelsea— or Chelski, as some now call it,' Marcus added dryly. He broke off quickly, but Ella did not need the sight of Marcus's most ingratiating smile to tell her that the man was close behind her. She could feel his presence. The spicy scent of his cologne assailed her senses, and the tiny hairs on the back of her neck stood on end when he spoke in a deep, melodious voice that was as rich and sensuous as the notes of a cello.

'Forgive my intrusion, but I would like to offer my congratulations to Miss Stafford on her performance tonight.'

'Mr Aleksandrov.' Marcus's hand shot past Ella's nose as he greeted the Russian. 'I'm Marcus Benning, Ella's publicist. And this, of course —' he patted Ella's shoulder in a faintly possessive manner '—is Lady Eleanor Stafford.'

Ella blushed, and felt a surge of irritation with Marcus, who knew she disliked using her title but insisted that it was a good marketing tool. But as she turned to face the man, Marcus, the other guests, everything faded, and only Vadim Aleksandrov existed. Her eyes flew to his face and her blush deepened at the feral gleam in his gaze. A curious mix of fear and excitement shot through her, together with the ridiculous feeling that her life would never be the same again after this moment. She felt a strange reluctance to shake his hand, and shock ripped through her when he lifted her fingers to his mouth and pressed his lips to her knuckles.

'Eleanor.' His accented gravelly voice sent the same quiver of pleasure down her spine that she felt when she drew her bow across the strings of her violin. The feather-light brush of his mouth against her skin burned as if he had branded her, and with a little gasp she snatched her hand back, her heart beating frantically beneath her ribs.

'It's an honour to meet you, Mr Aleksandrov,' Marcus said eagerly. 'Am I right that your company holds the monopoly on mobile phone sales in Russia?'

'We certainly took advantage of the gap in the communications market in its early days of trading, but the company has grown and diversified widely since then,' Vadim Aleksandrov murmured dismissively. He continued to stare intently at Ella, and Marcus finally took the hint.

'Where are all the damn waiters? I could do with a refill,' he muttered, waving his empty champagne glass before he wandered off towards the bar.

For a split second Ella was tempted to race after him, but the enigmatic Russian's brilliant blue eyes seemed to exert a magnetic hold over her, and she was so overwhelmed by his potent masculinity that she found herself rooted to the spot.

'You played superbly tonight.'

'Thank you.' She struggled to formulate a polite response, her whole being conscious of the electrical attraction that arced between them. She had never experienced anything like it before, never been so acutely aware of a man, and it was frankly terrifying.

Vadim's sardonic smile warned her that he recognised her awareness of him. 'I have never heard another non-Russian play Prokofiev with the passionate intensity for which he—and many of my countrymen—are renowned,' he murmured, in a crushed-velvet voice that seemed to enfold Ella in its intimate caress.

Was that a roundabout way of telling her that *he* was passionate? The thought came unbidden into her head, and colour flared along her cheekbones as she acknowledged that he had no need to point out what was so blindingly obvious—even to her, with her severely limited sexual experience. Vadim Aleksandrov wore his virility like a badge, and she found the bold appreciation in his eyes as he trailed them over her body deeply unsettling.

'Are you enjoying the party?'

Ella glanced around the packed reception room, where several hundred guests were all talking at once. The hubbub of voices hurt her ears. 'It's very nice,' she murmured.

The glint of amusement in Vadim's eyes told her he knew she was lying. 'I understand you are giving another performance tomorrow evening, so I assume you are staying in Paris?'

'Yes. At the Intercontinental,' she added when his brows lifted quizzically.

'I'm at the George V, not far from you. I have a car waiting outside—can I offer you a lift back to your hotel? Maybe we could have a drink together?'

'Thank you, but I can't rush away from the party,' Ella mumbled, aware that a couple of minutes ago she had planned to do just that. But Vadim Aleksandrov's blatant sensuality disturbed her composure far too much for her to contemplate socialising with him. The hungry look in his eyes warned her that he would expect a drink in the bar to lead to an invitation up to her room—and she was very definitely not the sort of woman who indulged in one-night stands.

But supposing she *had* been the sort of woman who invited a sexy stranger to spend the night with her? For a second her imagination ran riot, and a series of shocking images flashed into her mind, of Vadim undressing her and touching her body before he drew her down onto the crisp white sheets of her hotel bed and made love to her.

What *was* she thinking? She could feel the heat radiating from her face and hastily dropped her eyes from Vadim's speculative gaze, terrified that he might somehow have read her thoughts.

'The party is in your honour. Of course I understand your eagerness to remain,' he drawled in a faintly mocking tone. 'I'll be in London next week. Perhaps we could have dinner one evening?'

Ella swiftly dismissed the crazy impulse to accept his invitation. 'I'm afraid I'll be busy.'

'Every evening?' His sensual smile caused her heart to skip a beat. 'He's a lucky man.'

She frowned. 'Who is?'

'The lover who commands your attention every night.'

'I don't have a lover—' She stopped abruptly, realising that she had unwittingly revealed more about her personal life than she'd wished. The gleam of satisfaction in his eyes triggered alarm bells and she sent up a silent prayer of thanks when she caught sight of Marcus making signs for her to join him at the bar. 'If you'll excuse me, I think my publicist has arranged for me to give an interview.' She hesitated, while innate good manners battled with the urge to put as much distance as possible between herself and the disturbing Russian, and then said hurriedly, 'Thank you for the invitation, but music takes up all my time and I'm not dating at the moment.'

Vadim had moved imperceptibly closer, so that she could feel the heat emanating from his body. She stiffened, her eyes widening in shock when he reached out and stroked his finger lightly down her cheek. 'Then I shall just have to try and persuade you to change your mind,' he promised softly, before he turned and walked away, leaving her staring helplessly after him.

London—a week later

The Garden Room at Amesbury House buzzed with the murmur of voices as guests filed in and took their seats. The members of the Royal London Orchestra were already in their places, and there was the usual rustle of sheet music and a ripple of conversation from the musicians as they prepared for the concert.

Ella lifted her violin out of its case and gave a tiny shiver of pleasure as she ran her fingers over the smooth, polished maple. The Stradivarius was exquisite, and incredibly valuable. Several collectors had offered her a fortune for the rare instrument— more than enough for her to be able to buy somewhere to live and still leave her with a sizeable nest egg should her career falter. But the violin had belonged to her mother; its sentimental value was incalculable and she would never part with it.

She flicked through the music sheets on the stand in front of her, mentally running through the symphony, although she had little need of the pages of notes when she had put in four hours of practice that afternoon. Lost in her own world, she was only vaguely conscious of the voices around her until someone spoke her name.

'You're miles away, aren't you?' her fellow first violinist, Jenny March, said impatiently. 'I *said*, it looks as though one of us has an admirer—although sadly I don't think it's me,' she added, the note of genuine regret in her voice finally causing Ella to look up.

'Who do you mean?' she murmured, casting a curious glance around the room.

The orchestra had performed at Amesbury House in London's west end on several occasions. The Garden Room held an audience of two hundred, and provided a more intimate atmosphere than larger venues, but Ella preferred the anonymity of the Royal Albert Hall or the Festival Hall. Her eyes skimmed along the front row of guests and juddered to a halt on the figure sitting a few feet away from her.

'Oh! What's *he* doing here?' she muttered, jerking her head away seconds too late to avoid the familiar glinting gaze of the man who had plagued her dreams every night for the past week.

'You know him?' Jenny's eyes widened, and she could not disguise the hint of envy in her voice. 'What a dark horse you are, Ella. He's seriously gorgeous. Who is he?'

'His name is Vadim Aleksandrov,' Ella said in a clipped tone, aware that Jenny would badger her for information all night. 'He's a Russian billionaire. I've met him once— briefly—but I don't *know* him.'

'Well, it's obvious he'd like to get to know you,' Jenny said musingly, intrigued by the twin spots of colour staining Ella's cheeks. Lady Eleanor Stafford was renowned for being cool and composed—so much so that she had earned the nickname of ice princess by a few of the other orchestra members—but at this moment Ella was looking distinctly flustered.

'I can't understand why he's here,' Ella muttered tensely. 'According to the gossip column in the magazine I read, he's supposed to be at the film festival in Cannes with a famous Italian actress.' The photo of him and his voluptuous companion had lodged in Ella's mind, and to her annoyance she had been unable to forget it, nor dismiss the shocking image in her head of a naked Vadim making love to his latest mistress. His private life did not interest her, she reminded herself sharply. Vadim Aleksandrov did not interest her, and she absolutely would not give in to the urge to turn her head and meet the piercing blue gaze she sensed was focused on her.

But her prickling awareness of him did not lessen, and she had to force herself to concentrate as the audience settled and the RLO's principal conductor, Gustav Germaine, lifted his baton. She adored Dvorak's *New World Symphony*, and she was annoyed with herself for being distracted by Vadim's presence. Taking a deep breath, she positioned her violin beneath her chin, and only then, as she drew her bow, did she relax and give all her attention to the music that flowed from wood and strings and seemed to surge up inside her, obliterating every other thought.

An hour and a half later the last notes of the symphony faded and the sound of the audience's tumultuous applause shattered Ella's dream-like state, catapulting her back to reality.

'Good grief! Gustav's almost smiling,' Jenny whispered as the members of the orchestra stood and bowed. 'That must mean he's satisfied with our performance for once. Too right—it sounded pretty well perfect to me.'

'I wasn't entirely happy with the way I played at the start of the fourth movement,' Ella muttered.

'But you're even more of a perfectionist than Gustav,' Jenny said, unconcerned. 'From the audience's response, they loved it—especially your Russian. He hasn't taken his eyes off you the whole evening.'

'He's not *my* Russian.' Ella did not want to be reminded of Vadim Aleksandrov, or learn that he had been watching her. She certainly did not want to glance over in his direction, but, like a puppet tugged by invisible strings, she turned her head a fraction, her eyes drawn inexorably to the dark-haired figure in the front row.

Jenny was right—he was gorgeous, she admitted reluctantly. Music dominated her life, and usually she took little notice of men, but Vadim was impossible to ignore. He was tall—three or four inches over six feet tall by her estimation—with impressively broad shoulders sheathed in a superbly tailored dinner jacket. His jet-black hair and olive-toned complexion hinted at a Mediterranean ancestry, which made his vivid blue eyes beneath heavy black brows even more startling. His hard-boned face was exquisitely sculpted, with razor-sharp cheekbones, a patrician nose and a square chin that warned of a determined nature, while his beautifully shaped mouth was innately sensual.

Oh, yes—seriously gorgeous, and her reaction to him was seriously unnerving, Ella acknowledged, feeling her heart slam beneath her ribs when those blue eyes trailed over her in a leisurely inspection and his lips curved into an amused smile that warned her he was well aware of the effect he had on her.

'So, where did you meet a sexy Russian billionaire?' Jenny muttered beneath the sound of the audience's applause. 'And if you're not interested in him I think it's only fair you introduce him to me. He's practically edible.'

Jenny was irrepressible, and despite herself Ella's lips twitched. 'I met him in Paris.'

Jenny's eyes widened. 'Paris—the city of romance. This gets better and better. Did you sleep with him?'

'*No!* Absolutely not.' Ella gave her friend a scandalised glance. 'Do you think I'd jump into bed with a man I'd only just met?'

'Not normally, no.' Ella's coolness with members of the opposite sex was well known. 'But perhaps if he looked at you the way he's looking at you now…' Jenny murmured shrewdly.

Ella knew she was going to regret her next question. 'How is he looking at me?' she asked, striving to sound uninterested—and failing.

'Like he's imagining undressing you, very slowly, and stroking his hands over every inch of your body as he exposes you to his hungry gaze.'

'For heaven's sake, Jen! I don't know what kind of books you've been reading lately.'

Jenny watched Ella's face flood with colour and grinned. 'You asked—I'm just telling you what I reckon is in your Russian's mind.'

'*He's not my Russian.*' Ella took a deep breath, and by sheer effort of will did not glance over at Vadim—but she could not dismiss the memory of the searing attraction she had felt the first time she had met him. A force beyond her control demanded that she turn her head, and as her eyes clashed with his brilliant gaze she felt a fierce tug of sexual awareness in the pit of her stomach. To her horror she felt an exquisite tingling sensation in her breasts as her nipples hardened, and mortification swept through her when Vadim deliberately lowered his eyes to the stiff peaks straining beneath her clingy silk jersey dress. Scarlet-faced, she jerked her head away from him and by sheer effort of will forced her lips into a smile as she faced the audience and bowed once more.

Vadim felt a surge of satisfaction when he noted the betraying signs that Ella Stafford was not as immune to him as she would like him to believe. When they had met a week ago he had been blown away by her delicate beauty, and intrigued by her coolness. He wanted her badly—perhaps more than he had ever wanted a woman, he brooded as his eyes skimmed over her slender body, following the slight curve of her hips, the indent of her tiny waist and the delicate swell of her breasts beneath her black cocktail dress.

Her hair was swept up into an elegant chignon, and for a moment he indulged in the pleasurable fantasy of removing the pins so that the pale blonde silk fell around her shoulders. To his shock, he felt himself harden. He hadn't been this turned-on since he was a testosterone-fuelled youth, he acknowledged self-derisively, and he inhaled sharply, his nostrils flaring slightly as he imposed ruthless self-control over his hormones.

The members of the orchestra were now filing out of the Garden Room. He was aware that Ella had determinedly not looked in his direction, but as she stepped forward she shot him a lightning glance, and colour flared along her cheek-bones when he dipped his head in acknowledgement.

Her reaction pleased him. He had known when they had met in Paris and he had seen the flare of startled awareness in her eyes that the attraction was mutual. Sexual alchemy was a potent force that held them both in its grip, but for some reason she had refused his invitation to dinner in a cool tone that had been at variance with her dilated pupils and the tremulous softness of her mouth.

He dismissed the rumour circulating among certain individuals of her social group that she was frigid. No one could play an instrument with such fire and passion and have ice running through her veins. But her resistance was certainly a novelty. He had never before encountered a problem persuading any woman into his bed, Vadim mused cynically, aware that his billionaire status accounted for much of his attraction.

But Ella was different from the models and socialites he usually dated. She was a member of the British aristocracy; beautiful, intelligent and a gifted musician. The sexual attraction between them was indisputable, and as Vadim turned his head to watch her slender figure walk out of the Garden Room he felt a surge of determination to make her his mistress.

The evening at Amesbury House was a fundraising event organised by the patron of a children's charity, and after the performance by the RLO a selection of cheeses and fine wines were served in the Egyptian Room. Ella smiled and chatted with the guests, but she was conscious of the familiar empty feeling inside her that always followed a performance. She had put her heart and soul into playing, but now she felt emotionally drained, and the hubbub of voices exacerbated her niggling headache.

She had not seen Vadim since she had caught his amused

stare on her way out of the Garden Room, and she assumed that he had left immediately after the performance. It was a relief to know she would not have to contend with his disturbing presence for the rest of the evening, she thought as she stepped through the door leading to the orangery—a glass-roofed conservatory that ran the length of the house, and which was blessedly cool and quiet after the stuffy atmosphere of the Egyptian Room. It was beautiful here among the leafy citrus trees, but she longed to be back at Kingfisher House, beside the River Thames, her home for the past few years. She glanced at her watch, wondering how soon she could slip away from the party, and gave a startled gasp when a figure stepped out of the shadows.

'I thought you'd gone.' Shock lent a sharp edge to her voice, and Vadim Aleksandrov's dark brows rose quizzically.

'I am flattered that you noticed my absence, Lady Eleanor.'

His deep, accented voice was so innately sexy that she could not restrain the little shiver of reaction that ran through her. The only light in the orangery came from the silver moonbeams slanting through the glass, and she hoped he could not see the flush of colour that surged into her cheeks.

'Please don't call me that,' she said tautly. 'I never use my title.'

'You would prefer for me to call you Ella, as your friends do?' In the pearly grey half-light Vadim's smile revealed a set of perfect white teeth which reminded Ella of a predatory wolf. 'I am delighted that you regard me as a friend,' he drawled. 'It marks a major step forward in our relationship.'

She froze, infuriated by his mocking tone, and aware of an underlying serious note in his voice that warned her to be on her guard. 'We don't have a relationship to move forward, backward, or anywhere else,' she snapped.

'An unsatisfactory situation that can easily be remedied. I

have two tickets for *Madame Butterfly* at the Royal Opera House for Thursday evening. Would you care to join me? We could have dinner after the performance.'

'I'm flying to Cologne to play at the Opernhaus on Wednesday,' Ella told him truthfully, assuring herself that the faint twinge of regret she felt was only because Puccini's famous opera was one of her favourites.

Vadim shrugged, drawing her attention to the formidable width of his shoulders, and she felt a curious tugging sensation low in her stomach. 'I'll rearrange the tickets for another night.'

His supreme self-confidence was that of a man who was used to getting his own way, and his arrogant smile made Ella's hackles rise. Clearly he expected women to fall at his feet, and no doubt there were plenty who would leap at the chance to spend an evening with him—and then probably leap into his bed with the same eagerness—but she wasn't one of them. She had tried to rebuff him politely, but obviously blunter tactics were needed. 'Which part of *no* don't you understand?' she queried icily.

Far from seeming offended, he widened his smile and strolled towards her, his piercing blue gaze trapping her as helplessly as a rabbit confronted by car headlights. She was of average height, and her heels gave her the advantage of another three inches, but he still towered over her, the muscular strength of his chest a formidable barrier which barred her escape from the orangery. He had invaded her thoughts day and night for the past week, and now, as she inhaled the exotic tang of his cologne, her senses swam and she could not deny her agonising awareness of him.

'This part,' Vadim said softly, sliding his hand beneath her chin and lowering his head before she had time to comprehend his intention—or react to it.

CHAPTER TWO

'No!' ELLA's outraged gasp was muffled beneath the firm pressure of Vadim's mouth on hers, and shock rendered her immobile. His lips were warm and beguiling as he kissed her with an expertise that caused her heart to slam against her ribs. He moved his hand from her chin to her nape, while his other hand settled on her hip and urged her closer. He did not exert force, and she could easily resist—*should* resist, her brain pointed out—but her body seemed to have a will of its own, and it craved even closer contact with the most mesmeric man she had ever met.

His tongue traced the shape of her mouth, playing havoc with her equilibrium, but when he probed gently between her lips, demanding access, she stiffened and her pride belatedly stirred. She knew what kind of man he was. After meeting him in Paris she had been sufficiently intrigued to find out more about him, and had discovered that he had a reputation as a playboy whose wealth and undeniable charisma attracted women to his bed in droves. His relationships never lasted long before he moved on to his next conquest, and she would not be one of them, Ella vowed fiercely.

She did not want a love affair, and she was certain that love was not on Vadim's agenda. He wanted to have sex with her.

She might be inexperienced, but she was not completely naïve, and from the moment their eyes had met in Paris she had recognised the hungry desire in his gaze. He wanted her, but she was determined he would not have her. She'd never had a problem freezing out other men who had shown an interest in her, and the fact that she was finding it hard to remain cool with Vadim was all the more reason to stick to her resolve.

She knew about men like him, she brooded bitterly. Her father had repeatedly broken her mother's heart with his affairs. Even when Judith Stafford had lain dying the Earl had been cavorting with his mistress on the French Riviera, and had barely made it back to England in time for his wife's funeral.

But as Vadim continued his unhurried exploration of her lips she was aware of a curious melting sensation that seeped into her bones, undermining her determination to resist him, so that she could not prevent herself from sagging against him. His arm snaked around her waist, pulling her closer still, so that she could feel the solid hardness of his thigh muscles. In a frantic attempt to push him away she laid her hands flat against his chest, and was instantly entranced by the warmth of his body through his fine silk shirt.

Now he increased the pressure of his mouth, forcing her lips apart, and with a bold flick of his tongue he delved into her moist warmth, taking the kiss to another level and demonstrating a degree of eroticism that was beyond anything Ella had ever imagined. She felt strangely light-headed as her blood drummed through her veins, every nerve-ending in her body acutely sensitive, so that the faint rasp of his cheek against her tender flesh sent a quiver of reaction the length of her spine. Just as music transported her to another world, Vadim's kiss took her to a place she had never been before, where sensation ruled and all that mattered was that he should continue to move his mouth on hers in the slow, delicious tasting that caused a curious throbbing ache in the pit of her stomach.

She had no idea how long the kiss lasted. It could have been minutes, hours. While she was in his arms she lost all sense of time, and when at last he lifted his head and withdrew his hand from her waist she swayed slightly, the dazed expression in her eyes gradually changing to one of appalled self-disgust.

'How dare you?' she whispered through numbed lips, the realisation that she had capitulated utterly to his mastery sending shame cascading through her, so that her face flooded with hot colour.

He gave her an amused smile. 'How can you ask that after responding to me with such passion?' He ran his finger lightly over her flushed cheek, and then traced the swollen contours of her lips, his eyes darkening when he caught the faint catch of her breath. 'The word among some of your male friends is that you are frigid. But what do they know?' he murmured, his gravelly accent sounding deeper and more sensual than ever. 'They're just young bucks who are piqued that you have not chosen one of them to be your boyfriend. But you should not have boys, Ella. You need a man who appreciates your sensual nature.'

'Are you suggesting I need *you*?' she choked, seizing anger as a weapon to fight the insidious warmth that his sexy voice and provocative statement evoked inside her. The sultry gleam in his eyes was too much to bear. 'Your ego is…*monumental*. And I don't care what anyone thinks of me,' she added tightly.

She was aware of the speculation among the brothers of some of her friends that her refusal to date them must mean she was either frigid or gay. The true explanation was that she simply wasn't interested, but Vadim's suggestion that she had been holding out for a highly sexed, overconfident man like him—a man like her father—was laughable. She had made it clear that she wanted nothing to do with him, and it was his problem if his ego couldn't accept her refusal to have dinner with him.

She had given out a mixed message tonight, though, she conceded grimly, shuddering at the memory of how she had responded to him with shameful enthusiasm. She should have pulled away from him the moment he had touched her, but instead she had melted in his arms. Mortification swept through her, together with a growing sense of panic as Vadim traced his finger down her throat and continued lower, coming to rest on the faint swell of her breasts, visible above the neckline of her dress. Her breath hitched in her throat, and she was terrified that he must be able to see her heart jerking unevenly beneath her ribs. Every instinct screamed at her to slap his hand away, but to her shame a little part of her longed for him to move his fingers the few necessary inches to curve around her breast.

Her eyes flew to his face, and the feral gleam she saw beneath his heavy lids warned her he had read her mind. 'The game of cat and mouse has been amusing,' he said in his sinfully sexy accent, 'but now I grow bored with it. Perhaps you are shocked by the intensity of the sexual chemistry between us, Ella, but you cannot deny it exists. When we kissed, you felt it here.' He placed his hand directly over her heart, his fingers brushing against her breast. 'Just as I did. Passion pounds in your veins as it does in mine, and the only logical conclusion is for us to become lovers.'

She could not possibly be tempted, Ella told herself frantically. She was incensed by Vadim's arrogant assumption that she was his for the taking, that he could simply pluck her like a ripe peach, and yet she could not block out the little voice in her head which was urging her to agree, to succumb to the passion that, as he had rightly guessed, was pounding in her veins, making her feel hot and flustered.

Common sense fought the wild recklessness that had gripped her and won. She would not be Vadim Aleksandrov's *plaything*. She recalled a newspaper article about his recent split from glamour model Kelly Adams, in which Kelly had accused him of cruelly dumping her by text message. The accompanying photo had shown the stunning redhead sobbing heartbrokenly outside the hotel where Vadim had taken up residence since his arrival in the capital. 'Vadim Aleksandrov has a lump of granite instead of a heart,' Kelly had told the tabloids, and the image of the model's tear-streaked face had reminded Ella of her mother's anguished expression when Lionel Stafford had rejected her for one of his many mistresses.

'When you say lovers, what exactly do you have in mind?' she queried coolly. 'I know from press reports that you travel widely for your company, and I am frequently on tour with the RLO, so I'm not sure how we could maintain a meaningful relationship.'

He frowned, clearly taken aback by her words. 'To be honest, I had not thought that far ahead,' he drawled. 'I am suggesting that we explore the sexual attraction that exists between us, but talk of a relationship is a little premature, don't you think?'

Vadim Aleksandrov and the late Earl Stafford had a lot in common, Ella brooded, not least their cavalier attitude towards women. 'I might have known that a man like you would only be interested in physical satisfaction,' she said bitterly, forcing herself to sound coldly dismissive to disguise her intense awareness of him.

Vadim's eyes narrowed at her haughty tone. 'A man like me?' he queried softly. The expression on Ella's face was dismissive, scornful, and anger flared inside him. Did she think he was beneath her because he had started out in life with nothing, while she had been born into the wealthy, privileged lifestyle of the British upper class?

He was used to women who played games, and he had cynically assumed that Ella had been cool with him because it amused her. Now he wondered if her refusal to date him was because she deemed him a lowly immigrant from the Eastern bloc who had made a fast buck, not worthy of her. He assured himself he did not give a damn about her opinion of him, but to his annoyance his pride stung. 'What kind of a man do you think I am?' he demanded harshly.

As Ella stared at his hard-boned face her mind flew back across the years and she was back at Stafford Hall, huddled at the top of the stairs, peering through the banisters to the hall below, where her mother was sobbing as she pleaded with a cold, arrogantly handsome man.

'You're going to her *again, aren't you? Did you think I was unaware of your latest mistress when the whole of London knows you spend your nights with your tart instead of with me? For pity's sake, Lionel...'*

Judith Stafford lifted her hands beseechingly towards her husband, but there was no pity in the Earl's eyes, just cold indifference which turned to anger when his wife clutched the lapels of his jacket.

'Why on earth would I want to spend any more time than I have to with you? You're a neurotic, pathetic mess.' Lip curling with distaste, Lionel Stafford pushed the weeping woman away from him with such force that she stumbled and fell to her knees. 'Pull yourself together, Judith, and be thankful I go elsewhere for my pleasures when you consistently deny me my rights in the marriage bed.'

'I'm not well, Lionel. You know my heart condition means I have to be careful...'

'Well, I'm bored with your illness.' The Earl flung open the

*door and gave one last withering glance at his wife, still
kneeling on the cold marble floor. 'Don't wait up,' he said
mockingly. 'I don't know when I'll be back.'*

Ella remembered the anger that had surged through her as
her father had slammed the door behind him, and the pity and
the feeling of utter helplessness as she'd watched her mother
slowly drag herself to her feet and make her way wearily to
the stairs. At twelve years old she had been unable to voice
her hatred of her father, and less than a year later, after her
mother had died of heart failure, she had been packed off to
boarding school and left in the charge of a nanny during the
holidays, while the Earl disappeared abroad. Her resentment
had continued to fester inside her. Lionel Stafford had died
before Ella had had the opportunity to tell him how much she
hated him, but now, as she stared at Vadim's arrogant face, her
bitterness came tumbling out.

'I think you are the kind of man who selfishly takes what
you want and gives nothing in return. You have a reputation
as a playboy, but you have no respect for women.' She lifted
her head and glared at him, determined not to be fazed by the
mocking gaze that so infuriated her. But there was no amusement in those piercing blue eyes, just a feral gleam that made
her feel hot and shivery at the same time, and she had the
uncomfortable feeling that he could see inside her head.

Anger surged up inside her, making her tremble with its
intensity. How dared he make the casual suggestion that they
should become lovers? And how dared he kiss her with such
shocking hunger that he had forced her to respond to him
against her will? She could not drag her gaze from his mouth,
couldn't forget the sensual pleasure of his lips sliding over
hers, but no way did she want him to kiss her again—of
course she didn't, she assured herself fiercely.

'I'd rather die than have you touch me again.' As soon as

the words were out she knew she'd sounded childish and overdramatic, and her blush deepened when he gave her an amused glance.

'If I thought you really meant it I would walk away and never trouble you again,' he said softly. 'But we both know it isn't true. You desire me as much as I want you, and have done since the moment we met in Paris. The attraction between us was instant, like wildfire, but you don't have the guts to be honest about it.'

Incensed, she stared at him, shaking with rage, and yet deep down she was aware of a need to goad him, to make him do…what? 'How can you possibly think you know my mind better than I do?' she gritted.

'I know you want me to kiss you again.' His voice was suddenly rough, the amusement in his eyes replaced by scorching heat. 'Let's try a little experiment, shall we?' His arm shot out and he jerked her against him, ignoring her struggles to escape with insulting ease as he lowered his mouth to hers.

There was no gentleness this time, just raw, primitive passion as he took without mercy, forcing her lips apart with a bold flick of his tongue before he thrust deep into her moist warmth and explored her with ruthless efficiency. Fighting him was impossible when his arms were clamped like a vice around her body. But she did not have to respond to him, her brain pointed out. She could simply remain passive until he'd finished with her. But, to her shame, her willpower was non-existent, and the delicious pressure of his mouth proved an irresistible temptation.

It was ridiculous that at twenty-four she did not know how to kiss a man properly, Ella mused. But her music consumed her so utterly that she had never felt more than mild curiosity about the opposite sex, and on the rare occasions she had agreed to go on a date she had found the obligatory fumbling kiss in the car, with the gear lever jammed into her ribs, totally uninspiring.

Being kissed by Vadim was a completely different experience. He was a master in the art of seduction, while she was dangerously out of her depth. The erotic sweep of his tongue destroyed her thought processes, and she gave up trying to deny him when it meant denying herself, initiating a tentative exploration of her own that elicited a low groan from him as he felt her complete capitulation.

She was flushed and breathless when he finally released her. 'You see—you survived,' he taunted softly.

Ella wished she could make some cutting retort, but her brain seemed to have stopped functioning. Her lips felt swollen when she traced them with her tongue, and she doubted she could have uttered a word.

Vadim's eyes darkened as he watched the darting foray of her pink tongue-tip, and he muttered something she assumed was Russian as he made to pull her back into his arms. But suddenly, shockingly, the orangery was flooded with a brilliant glare as someone pushed open the door and flicked the light switch.

'Oh…sorry.' Jenny did not bother to disguise her curiosity as she watched Ella flush scarlet and spring away from the gorgeous Russian hunk who had been eyeing her up all night. 'Ella, there's been a mix-up with the taxis. They've only sent one car, and Claire's cello will take up half the back seat. The driver says he'll come back for you after he's driven us home, as you live in the opposite direction. Do you mind waiting?'

'No, that's fine.' Ella forced a smile, despite the sudden feeling that her head was about to explode. The migraine she had sensed brewing earlier had kicked in with a vengeance, the pain escalating as quickly as it always did with her, so that she could barely concentrate on anything else. She refused to make a fuss about the travel arrangements, even though the prospect of waiting around for her lift home seemed unbearable when a dozen hammers were beating against her skull. She supposed she could ring another cab company, but moving her head even slightly was agony, and she was conscious of the unpleasant queasy sensation in her stomach that usually preceded a bout of sickness.

'Are you okay?' Jenny's voice sounded like a pneumatic drill to Ella's ultra-sensitive ears. 'You look a bit green.'

Somehow Ella managed another faint smile. 'A headache. It's nothing. You'd better go, or the taxi will leave without you.'

Jenny hesitated, frowning at Ella's sudden pallor. 'Are you sure?'

'I'll take Ella home.' Vadim's deep voice was firm and decisive, and at any other time she would have railed against his authority, but right now getting home as fast as possible was imperative, so she nodded her head very slightly, trying not to wince as stars flashed in front of her eyes.

'Thank you.' She sensed his surprise at her sudden meekness, but the pain was worse, blinding her, so that she stumbled after him, back through the Egyptian Room and out to the foyer, where she collected her violin from the security desk and then followed Vadim out onto the street. She'd hoped that a few gulps of fresh air would lessen the nauseous feeling, but if anything she felt worse, and after easing carefully into his low-slung sports car, and muttering instructions on how to reach her house, she closed her eyes and prayed she would not throw up over his leather upholstery.

If there was one thing Vadim couldn't stand it was a woman who sulked. He did not even know why he was bothering with Ella, he thought grimly, after his attempts at conversation were met with a barely monosyllabic response. He took his eye off the road for a second and threw her an impatient glance, his mouth tightening when he saw that she had turned her head away from him and was staring fixedly out of the window. He knew of half a dozen extremely attractive women he could phone who would be happy to provide a few hours of pleasant company and uncomplicated sex. So why was he hung up on this pale, underweight girl, who changed from hot to cold quicker than a mixer-tap, and was now subjecting him to the big freeze because he had proved that she was sexually attracted to him?

Her coolness intrigued him, he admitted, particularly now he had sampled the heated passion she kept hidden behind her ice-maiden façade. But his attempts to get Ella to have dinner with him, let alone persuade her into his bed, had so far come to nothing, and he was beginning to wonder if she was worth the effort. Maybe he should drop her home and put her out of his mind? His hectic work schedule meant that he hadn't had a lover for weeks. Celibacy did not agree with him, he acknowledged self-derisively. But Ella Stafford was too much like hard work.

'Stop the car,' she cried suddenly.

He frowned. 'According to the sat-nav we're still a mile from your address.'

'Just stop the car *now*. Please.'

The urgency in her voice puzzled him. Did she want him to leave her at the side of the road because she was afraid that if he drove her all the way home he might demand an invitation into her house? He swore violently in his native tongue and pulled up in a lay-by, his frown deepening when she immediately shot out of the car and raced towards the bushes a few feet back from the road.

'Ella…?'

'Don't follow me,' she yelled.

He swore again. God damn it, what did she think he was going to do to her? He swung back to the car and then paused at the unmistakable sound of retching coming from the bushes. A few minutes later she reappeared, whey-faced, her eyes like great hollows in her pinched face. She looked like death, and his impatience faded as some indefinable emotion tugged in his chest.

'What the hell is the matter with you?'

'Migraine.' Ella forced the word past her chattering teeth, took one look at Vadim's horrified expression and wanted to die of embarrassment. There was no hint of desire in his eyes now, she noted grimly, but that was hardly surprising when he had just heard her lose the contents of her stomach. 'I occasionally get them after a performance. Playing is incredibly draining, and it seems that a surfeit of emotions affects me physically.' She leaned weakly against the car, wondering if he would allow her to get back in, or whether he expected her to walk the remaining distance to her house for fear that she would be sick again. 'You're partly to blame,' she muttered, not daring to look at him and see the disgust he must surely feel. 'You unsettle me.'

He gave a rough laugh, but when he spoke the anger had gone from his voice. 'Honesty at last! If it's any consolation, you unsettle me too. But I'm not sure I like the idea that I make you physically ill.'

'You don't…I mean, it wasn't you…' Why on earth had she admitted that he unsettled her? Ella asked herself crossly. She was naturally reserved—a trait that was frequently mistaken for aloofness—and she hated the nickname she'd earned of Ice Princess, but right now she would give anything to appear cool and collected. 'I find Dvorak's *New World Symphony* very emotional to play,' she muttered, colour flaring on her white face.

'I'm relieved to know that my kissing you did not make you sick.' There was amusement in Vadim's voice now and Ella glared at him, or tried to, but the pain across her temples was excruciating and she closed her eyes, wishing she were back home at Kingfisher House rather than standing by the side of the road with a man who infuriated her and fascinated her in equal measures.

'Do you have medication for your headache?'

She forced her eyes open to find him standing close beside her, and for some inexplicable reason she wanted to rest her pounding head against the broad strength of his chest. 'My prescription painkillers are at home. I usually carry some with me, but I forgot them tonight,' she muttered ruefully.

'Then I'd better get you home quickly.' Vadim helped her into the car and strode round to the driver's side, coiling his long frame behind the wheel. 'Here, let me do that.' He leaned across her and adjusted her seat belt, and despite the throbbing pain in her head Ella was acutely conscious of his closeness, her senses flaring as she breathed in the subtle scent of his cologne.

In the glow from the street-lamp his swarthy olive skin gleamed like silk, but the brilliance of his blue eyes was shielded by thick black lashes. His mouth was inches from hers, and she recalled the firm pressure of his lips easing hers apart, demanding a response she had been helpless to deny. She suddenly felt hot, when seconds ago she had been freezing cold, but she could not blame her erratic temperature swing on her migraine, she admitted dismally. For some reason this man affected her in a way no man had ever done—made her feel things she had confidently assumed would never trouble her.

When Vadim had told her that some of her male friends thought she was frigid, she hadn't been surprised. It had occurred to her that the reason for her complete lack of interest in the opposite sex might not only be due to the hatred she had felt for her father, and that she must simply have a low sex-drive. But the erotic dreams that had plagued her since this Russian had first kissed her hand in Paris had turned that notion on its head. He had awoken her sensuality—but far from wanting to explore the feelings he aroused in her—her instinct was to run and keep on running.

Vadim stared at her, and said in a half-amused, half-impatient voice, 'For pity's sake, don't look at me like that *now*, when you know damn well there's nothing I can do about it.'

'Like what?' she mumbled, dazed with pain and overwhelmed by his potent masculinity.

'Like you want me to kiss you again and keep on kissing you, until the slide of mouth on mouth is no longer enough for either of us and only the feel of hands caressing naked skin will satisfy the ache that consumes us both,' he said, in a low tone that simmered with sexual promise.

Face burning at the images he evoked, Ella jerked upright—and drew a sharp breath when a burning poker pierced her skull. 'I didn't...I don't...'

'Liar.'

She was so pale she looked as though she might pass out. Vadim controlled his frustration and fired the ignition, wondering how he could ever have bought into the image Ella projected of cool, reserved, independent woman. Instead she was a seething mass of emotions, intense, hot-blooded and surprisingly vulnerable, and she intrigued him more than any other woman had ever done. Walking away from her was not an option right now, he conceded grimly. He wanted her, and he knew damn well that she wanted him; he simply had to convince her of that fact.

But now was not the time, he acknowledged when he shot

another glance at her wan face. She looked achingly fragile, and he was surprised by the level of his concern. He drove along the main road until the satellite navigation system instructed him to take a right turn into a side street which he suddenly realised was familiar, and his frown deepened when he swung onto the driveway of a large, beautiful mansion house.

'*This* is your house?' he queried harshly.

'I wish,' Ella muttered, too overwhelmed by the pain in her head to wonder why Vadim sounded puzzled. 'It belongs to my uncle. He owns an estate agency business, and when Kingfisher House came onto the market a few years ago he snapped it up as an investment. He rents the main part of the house out to tenants, and I live in the adjoining staff quarters and act as caretaker when the house is empty—as it has been for the past couple of months.' She climbed out of the car and glanced wistfully at the gracious old house that she had fallen in love with the minute she'd first seen it. 'Hopefully when Uncle Rex finds new tenants they'll allow me to continue living here.' The American businessman who had rented Kingfisher House the previous year had travelled extensively with his job, and had been happy for Ella to stay and keep an eye on the place, but new people might want to use the staff quarters, which would mean she would have to move out. The possibility of having to find somewhere else to live had been worrying her for weeks, but right now all she could think of was swallowing a couple of painkillers and crawling into bed, and so she started to walk carefully towards the front door on legs that felt decidedly wobbly.

Strong arms suddenly closed around her, and she gave a startled cry when Vadim swung her into his arms. 'Stop fighting and let me help you,' he said roughly. 'You're about to collapse.' Her eyes were shadowed with pain, and the shimmer of tears evoked another tug of compassion that surprised him when usually he had little patience for weakness. His childhood had been tough, and devoid of kindness, and two years doing his national service in the Russian army had been brutally harsh. He had learned early in life that survival was dependent on physical and mental strength, and he acknowledged the truth in the accusation by some of his ex-lovers that he was hard and unemotional.

He'd spent so long suppressing his feelings that it came as a shock to realise he had the capacity to feel pity; Vadim brooded as he strode up to the house. But for some reason the woman in his arms elicited an emotion in him that might almost be described as tenderness. His mouth tightened. The idea that he was drawn to Ella by anything more than sexual attraction was disturbing, and he swiftly rejected it. All he asked from the women who briefly shared his life was physical satisfaction—the slaking of mutual lust until desire faded and he grew bored and moved on to someone new. Ella was no different, he told himself grimly. He wanted her, and soon he would have her. But the beginning would spell the end, as it always did.

CHAPTER THREE

'YOU can put me down now,' Ella insisted, the moment Vadim had pushed open the front door and carried her across the entrance hall towards the sweeping staircase which led to the upper floors. 'My part of the house is on the ground floor, through that door. I'll manage fine, thank you,' she added tersely, when he did not set her down as she had hoped, but turned towards the door she had indicated.

He shouldered the door and strode into her sitting room, glancing around the spacious room which was dominated by an enormous grand piano. The room was at the back of the house, and through the French windows he could make out a sweeping lawn and beyond it the wide expanse of the River Thames, gleaming dully in the moonlight.

'You must have a wonderful view of the river.'

'Oh, yes, and of Hampton Court on the opposite bank. I love it here,' Ella confessed. 'I can't bear the thought that I may have to move out. It was very good of Uncle Rex to persuade his previous tenant to allow me stay here, but I might not be so lucky next time. The trouble is, there aren't many flats that I can afford with rooms big enough for the piano, or where I can practise my music for hours on end without disturbing the neighbours.'

'Why don't you sell the piano? My knowledge of musical instruments is limited, but I know Steinways are worth a fortune.'

'I'll never sell it,' Ella said fiercely. 'It was my mother's. She loved it, and it was one of the few possessions of hers I fought to keep when I had to sell Stafford Hall. That was the family pile,' she explained, when Vadim gave her a querying look. 'Stafford Hall was a gift to one of my ancestors from Henry VIII, and the house, along with a sizeable fortune, was passed down through the family for generations—until it reached my father.'

The undisguised bitterness in her voice stirred Vadim's curiosity. 'What happened? And where are your parents now?'

'They're both dead. My mother died when I was thirteen,' she revealed in a low tone, which hardened as she added, 'My father died five years ago—after he'd drunk and gambled away all the money. When it ran out he went though the house and sold off anything of value, but fortunately my mother had bequeathed her violin and piano to me in her will, and he wasn't able to touch them. After he died I had to sell the Hall to clear the mountain of debts he'd left, and that's when Uncle Rex allowed me to move in here.'

The Stafford fortune had not only been wasted on the late Earl's love of whisky and the roulette wheel but also on his love of women, Ella thought bitterly. Her father had been a notorious playboy, and from early childhood she had vowed never to be attracted to the type of man who treated women as a form of entertainment.

So why, she asked herself angrily, had she allowed Vadim Aleksandrov—a man who changed his mistresses more often than most men changed their socks—to kiss her tonight? And, even worse, why had she responded to him—perhaps given him the idea that she was willing to hop into bed with him?

The searing pain of her migraine was no excuse for her to

have weakly let him carry her into the house. She was acutely conscious of the feel of his arms around her waist and beneath her knees. Held close against his chest, she could hear the steady beat of his heart beneath her ear. It made her feel safe somehow, secure, but that was an illusion, of course, because the last thing she would be with Vadim was *safe*. He was a man like her father, a handsome heartbreaker, and from the moment she had met him her instincts had warned her to steer clear of him.

'Put me down, please.' She moved restlessly in his arms, but he ignored her struggles and strode across the sitting room to the door which stood ajar to reveal her bedroom.

'Where are your painkillers?'

'In the bedside drawer.' He lowered her slowly onto the bed, but the movement caused her to draw a sharp breath as the pain in her head became unendurable. She moaned when he flicked on the lamp, and as soon as he'd found her medication he doused the light so that the only illumination in the room was from the moonlight glimmering through the open curtains.

'I'll get you some water.'

She heard him walk into the *en suite* bathroom, and he returned seconds later to hand her a glass of water. The safety lid on the painkillers was beyond her, and she was grateful when he opened it and tipped two tablets into her palm. They were strong, and she knew that in ten minutes, fifteen at most, she would sink into oblivion and escape from the pain that was making her feel so sick.

'Can you see yourself out?' she whispered as she sank back against the pillows.

'I will, once you're in bed.' Vadim's velvet-soft voice was strangely soothing, and she closed her eyes, only to open them again with a jolt when she felt his hand on her ankle.

'What are you doing?'

'Taking your shoes off.' He sounded faintly amused. 'You can't get into bed wearing stiletto heels.'

How could the feel of his hands lightly brushing the soles of her feet as he removed her shoes be so intensely erotic? Ella wondered fretfully. Even in the throes of an agonising migraine she was desperately aware of him, and she could only pray he had not noticed the tremor that ran through her.

'Now your dress.'

'No way are you going to take my dress off.' She glared at him through pain-glazed eyes, daring him to touch her, but he ignored her and rolled her gently onto her side, so that he could slide her zip down her spine.

'You're telling me you can undress yourself?' He took her fulminating silence as a no, and, with a deftness she assumed he'd gained from regularly removing women's clothes, drew her dress over her shoulders and down to her waist. Arguing with him was impossible when her head was about to explode. More than anything she wanted to go to sleep and blot out the pain, and when he told her to lift her hips she obeyed, and allowed him to slide her dress down her legs. She didn't even care that he could see her functional black bra and knickers. Shivering with pain, she was past caring about anything, but when he drew the covers over her and stood up, good manners prompted her to speak.

'Thank you for bringing me home.'

Ella looked achingly fragile, and the fact that she hadn't fought him like a wildcat when he had removed her dress was an indication of the severity of her headache, Vadim mused wryly. 'Do your migraines usually last long?'

'I should be fine in the morning, hopefully,' Ella mumbled sleepily, her eyelids already feeling heavy as the painkillers began to work.

'Good. As for thanking me, you can do that when you have dinner with me next week.'

It took a few seconds for his words to sink in, and when she forced her eyes open he was already on his way out of the door. 'I told you, I'm going to Germany next week,' she called after him.

He glanced over his shoulder, and his sensual smile made her heart lurch. 'But you're back at the weekend. I checked with one of the other members of the orchestra. I'll be in touch.'

Ella didn't know whether to take that as a threat or a promise, but he had strolled out of her room and closed the door quietly behind him while she was still trying to think of another excuse. Irritating man, she thought angrily as she settled back on her pillow. But as she teetered on the edge of sleep she reminded herself that his ability to disturb her equilibrium also made him a dangerous man, and she was utterly determined not to have dinner with him.

Ella had completely recovered from her debilitating migraine by the time she flew to Cologne with the RLO. She had visited the city many times before, and instead of joining Jenny on a sightseeing trip she made up for her lost practice time by rehearsing for several hours before the concert. The programme of concertos by Bach and Beethoven was received with much acclaim; the orchestra received excellent reviews and arrived back at Gatwick on Saturday morning.

'I wouldn't mind being greeted with a bouquet of flowers,' Jenny commented enviously as they walked through the arrivals gate and spotted a courier clutching a huge arrangement of red roses.

Ella watched the courier talking to one of the orchestra members up ahead, and she gave Jenny a puzzled glance when he walked purposefully in their direction.

'Eleanor Stafford? These are for you.'

Struggling to hold her violin and suitcase, as well as the bouquet that had been thrust into her arms, Ella was nonplussed. 'There must be a mistake…'

'Open the card. Here…' Jenny rescued the violin, and with fumbling fingers Ella ripped open the envelope and read the note inside.

Welcome home, Ella. Dinner tonight, 7 p.m. I'll pick you up from Kingfisher House.

It was signed 'Vadim', and the sight of the bold black scrawl filled Ella with a mixture of annoyance and jittery excitement that she swiftly quashed. 'He hasn't even left a phone number so that I can cancel,' she noted irritably.

Jenny gave her a look that told Ella she was seriously questioning her sanity. 'Why would you want to? He's incredibly good-looking, mega-rich and as sexy as sin,' she listed. 'And he's sent you two dozen red roses. What more do you want? This guy is clearly keen.'

'I don't want anything from him,' Ella snapped. 'And all he wants is to take me to bed.'

'So, what's wrong with that?' Jenny stopped dead on the way out of the airport terminal and stared at Ella. 'You've always said—right back from when we were pig-tailed first-years at boarding school—that you never wanted to get married.'

'I don't.' Ella frowned, wondering where the conversation was leading.

'But you're saying you don't want an affair either? What are you going to do—live like a nun for the rest of your life?'

'Yes—no—I don't know,' Ella muttered. They had been friends for over a decade, and Jenny knew her better than anyone, but she couldn't explain her violent reaction to Vadim when she didn't understand it herself. 'Are you advocating that I should become Vadim Aleksandrov's plaything?' she demanded tersely.

'I can think of worse fates,' Jenny said cheerfully. 'Seriously, Ella…' Her smile faded. 'I know you didn't get on with your dad, and that he treated your mum badly, but you can't cut yourself off from the world, from men and relationships, because your parents' marriage didn't work out.'

'I haven't.' Ella defended herself tersely, but she knew deep down that she was lying. Jenny didn't understand. How could she, when her parents had been married for thirty years and her father was a gentle, kindly man who patently adored his wife and four children. Ella had spent many happy school holidays with Jenny and her family, and would have gladly swapped the lonely grandeur of Stafford Hall for the Marches' cramped bungalow in Milton Keynes, which was full of love and laughter. Jenny had no idea what it had been like to witness her father destroy her mother with his mental and sometimes physical cruelty, but the emotional scars ran deep in Ella's mind, and she had promised herself she would never put herself in a position where a man had any kind of hold over her.

'When was the last time you went on a date?' Jenny demanded.

Ella shrugged. 'A couple of months ago, actually. I had dinner with the flautist Michail Danowski when the Polish orchestra visited.'

Jenny gave her a look of mingled pity and exasperation. 'He's gay, so he doesn't count.'

Ella was saved from answering when a taxi drew up, and they spent the next few minutes stowing violins and luggage in the boot. 'You can't put those in here; they'll get crushed,' Jenny said when Ella crammed Vadim's flowers on top of her case. The roses were beautiful, she conceded when the taxi finally pulled away, and she stared at the bouquet on her lap. The velvety petals were a rich ruby-red, filling the car with their sensual perfume.

Red roses were for lovers; the thought stole into her mind together with Jenny's taunt about spending the rest of her life as a nun. Of course she wasn't going to do that, she assured herself. It was just that music and her career, both with the RLO and as a soloist, took up all her time, and she couldn't fit in a relationship right now. Not that Vadim was offering a relationship—he had admitted as much when he had kissed her at Amesbury House. All he wanted was an affair, and she refused to be another notch on his overcrowded bedpost.

The sight of Kingfisher House and the weeping cherry trees that lined the drive, bathed in spring sunshine, lifted Ella's spirits, and she couldn't wait to throw open the French doors at the back of the house and walk down the lawn to the private jetty beside the majestic River Thames. But first there was the usual pile of mail to deal with, and a message on the answer-machine drained all the pleasure from her homecoming.

'Ella, Uncle Rex here. I've found a new tenant for Kingfisher House. He's interested in buying the place, but he wants to rent it for six months to see whether it's suitable for him. There's no rush for you to move out. He's happy for you to stay on in the caretaker flat until he decides what he's going to do. I'll give you another call to arrange a time when you can meet him—hopefully some time this weekend.'

Ella's heart sank. She'd known that her uncle had been thinking of selling Kingfisher House, now that the high-end property market was improving after the downturn of the previous couple of years, but she'd put it out of her mind. Now it seemed likely that she would have to move within the next few months, and the problem of finding somewhere to live with rooms big enough to fit a concert grand piano would not make flat-hunting easy.

Life suddenly seemed full of uncertainty, and the prospect of seeing Vadim again added to her tension. She spent the rest of the day in a state of nervous apprehension, which grew worse as seven o'clock drew nearer. She was sure he had deliberately not included his phone number on his dinner invitation to prevent her from cancelling, but if he thought she was the type of woman who would meekly allow herself to be dominated by him, he'd better think again. No man was ever going to boss her around, she resolved fiercely, ignoring the twinge of her conscience that pointed out that it had been good of him to drive her home when she'd been in agony with a migraine. Colour flared on her cheeks when she recalled how he had removed her dress. But, far from taking advantage of her in her vulnerable state, Vadim had behaved like a gentleman and tucked her into bed.

Damn it, *why* couldn't he get the message that she wanted nothing to do with him? she brooded irritably as she arranged the mass of red roses in a vase. She didn't want him to send her flowers, but they were so beautiful that she couldn't bring herself to throw them in the bin. Most women would be delighted to receive roses from a gorgeous billionaire, she acknowledged ruefully, thinking of her conversation with Jenny. But she was not most women, and although she had denied it to Jenny, she knew that the fear and hatred she'd felt for her father continued to influence the way she felt about all men.

As usual when she felt tense, music was her salvation. She was building a successful career as a violinist, but she still played the piano purely for pleasure, and she was soon lost in another world as she moved her fingers over the smooth ivory keys, finding a release for her pent-up emotions in her favourite pieces by Chopin and Tchaikovsky.

* * *

Vadim was met by the haunting melody of Beethoven's *Moonlight Sonata* as he climbed out of his car and strode up the drive of Kingfisher House. He paused to listen, and felt the hairs on the back of his neck stand on end. Ella possessed a truly remarkable gift, and her brilliance as a musician fascinated him as much as her delicate beauty stirred his desire. Loath to disturb her by knocking on the front door, he walked around to the back of the house, where the French windows were thrown wide open and the lilting notes drifted on the air.

She was totally absorbed, and did not look up as he lowered himself onto one of the patio chairs, leaned back and closed his eyes, shutting out everything but the music. He had never played an instrument in his life; luxuries such as music lessons had not been affordable during his childhood, growing up in what had at that time been the USSR. His father's job as a factory worker had barely brought in enough money to pay the rent on the tiny apartment they had shared with Vadim's grandmother, and life had been dominated by the struggle to buy enough to eat during the frequent food shortages. He knew little about the great composers, or of musical techniques, but for some reason music had the power to soothe his restless soul, to reach deep inside him and force a chink in the granite wall around his heart.

As the last lingering notes of the melody faded Ella flexed her fingers, suddenly aware that the room was no longer flooded with afternoon sunlight, but shadowed with the onset of dusk.

'You play like an angel.'

The familiar, toe-curlingly sexy accent caused her to jerk her head towards the French windows, and her heart thudded beneath her ribs as she jumped to her feet and stared at Vadim.

'How long have you been there?' Shock at his appearance sharpened her voice. Playing the piano was an intensely personal experience, a special link with her mother, and she had poured her soul into the music. She had been unaware that she had an audience, and she felt as though she had unwittingly exposed her private emotions to Vadim.

He shrugged and stepped into the room. 'Twenty minutes or so.' His brilliant blue gaze skimmed over her tee shirt and faded jeans, and moved up to her hair, falling in a curtain of pale gold silk around her shoulders. This was the Ella Stafford the world did not see. Over the past few years she had been expertly marketed as a violin virtuoso; much had been made of her aristocratic pedigree, and she was portrayed on the covers of her numerous CD albums as a sophisticated artiste. The woman staring at him across the grand piano looked younger than her public image, and her intense awareness of him that flared, undisguised, in her stormy grey eyes made her seem painfully vulnerable.

A kinder man would not take his pursuit of her any further, Vadim knew. Beneath her ice-cool image he sensed an emotional fragility that warned him not to get involved. He liked his affairs to be uncomplicated, and he ensured that the women he bedded always knew the score: mutually satisfying sex with no strings attached. Ella seemed curiously innocent, although in reality that was unlikely for a modern and successful woman in her mid-twenties, he reminded himself. Seeing her like this, in jeans that moulded her slender hips like a second skin, her face bare of make-up and her hair falling loose to halfway down her back, only intensified his desire for her.

The sexual chemistry between them was white-hot, and kindness was not an attribute he possessed—he had learned that of himself many years ago, Vadim acknowledged grimly. He was hard; undoubtedly he was selfish, and he took what he wanted without compunction or compassion. He would take Ella because he found her pale, elfin beauty irresistible, but he would accept no responsibility for her emotions once he had slaked his hunger to possess her body.

'I had no idea you could play the piano with the same skill with which you play the violin.'

Ella shrugged. 'I don't play to performance standard. My mother was an astounding pianist. She could have had a wonderful career; should have done, but—' She broke off abruptly, feeling the familiar pain in her heart as she recalled her mother's gentle smile and her unending patience when she had tutored her daughter to play. Instead of enjoying the glittering career as a pianist that she had deserved, Judith Stafford had fallen in love and sacrificed her ambitions for a husband who had expected her to devote her life to being his social hostess. In return the Earl had broken her heart with his brazen infidelity. She would not make the same mistake as her mother, Ella vowed. And she would certainly never fall in love after she'd witnessed the devastation it caused.

Vadim flicked back the cuff of his jacket to glance at his watch, and Ella felt a peculiar sensation in the pit of her stomach when she glimpsed his olive-skinned wrist overlaid with dark hairs. He was so innately male, and so big, his broad shoulders sheathed in a black Armani jacket that he wore with the easy grace of a man who possessed supreme self-confidence.

She was conscious of his brief appraisal of her jeans, and blushed at his faintly sardonic smile. 'I assume you lost track of time. I'll phone the restaurant and tell them to hold our table while you get changed.'

She snatched a breath and said quietly, 'If you had given me a contact number, I would have phoned to explain that I'm unable to have dinner with you tonight—' she hesitated '—or any other night. This is a very busy time for me right now,' she added quickly, her blush deepening beneath his cool stare.

'But you do find time in your hectic schedule to eat, I take it?' he drawled. 'Although from what I saw of your body the other night, you clearly don't eat enough.'

'Well, I'm sorry if you found me a disappointment,' Ella snapped, infuriated by his reference to the embarrassing episode she would prefer to forget. If she hadn't been in such acute agony that night she wouldn't have allowed him to lay a finger on her, let alone undress her. As it was, Vadim had helped her out of her dress, but from the sound of it the sight of her bony figure and pathetically small breasts had not sent him wild with desire. A good thing too, she assured herself, suppressing a stupid wish that she possessed voluptuous curves like his glamorous ex-mistress Kelly Adams. She did not *want* Vadim to be interested in her, and perhaps now he'd discovered that she had the allure of a stick-insect he would leave her alone.

'I didn't say I found you disappointing,' he murmured, the sudden gleam in his eyes causing her heart to miss a beat as he strolled towards her. He was impossibly handsome, she recognised numbly, unable to tear her gaze from his sculpted features. The razor-sharp edges of his cheekbones and the hard planes of his face were cruelly beautiful, softened only slightly by the sensual curve of his mouth. He was almost unreal—like a marble figurine by one of the Old Masters, or one of those male models from the glossy magazines, who had been airbrushed to perfection. But Vadim was very real, a flesh-and-blood man who was standing unnervingly close to her, so that she could see the tiny lines that fanned around his piercing blue eyes.

'You know I am attracted to you. I have made no secret that I desire you,' he said, in such a bland tone that he might have been discussing the weather. But the expression in his eyes wasn't cool, it was scorching hot, and Ella caught her breath when he slipped his hand beneath her chin and lowered his head.

'But I'm not…I don't want…' She trailed off helplessly, transfixed by his mouth hovering tantalisingly close to hers.

'You don't want to date? Perhaps not other men,' he conceded arrogantly, 'but I'm different. I unsettle you,' he reminded her when she opened her mouth to argue, and then took advantage of her parted lips by covering them with his own and kissing her with a ruthless efficiency that blew her mind.

An instinct for self-protection warned Ella to resist, to freeze in Vadim's arms and jerk her head away so that he was denied access to her mouth. But another instinct, as old as womankind, caused molten heat to flood through her veins and evoked a shocking hunger inside her that was new and terrifying and yet utterly consuming. She wanted him to kiss her, taunted a voice in her head. For the past week she had been unable to forget the demanding pressure of his mouth on hers when he had kissed her at Amesbury House, and her dreams had been full of erotic images of what might have happened if they had not been disturbed. Now those dreams were reality, and his lips were once again working their sensual magic, coaxing her response until she opened her mouth for him and he thrust his tongue deep into her moist warmth.

No man had ever kissed her the way Vadim was doing. In the past she had dated a couple of musicians from the RLO, but her innate wariness made her seem cold and uninterested, and the relationships had quickly petered out. With Vadim it was different. He seemed to view her diffidence as a challenge, and had bulldozed through her defences to awaken her sensuality. For the first time in her life Ella felt the piercing intensity of sexual desire, and any idea of resisting its lure flew out of her mind as she sagged against the solid wall of his chest and felt his arms tighten around her.

He slid one hand into her hair and tugged, angling her head and deepening the kiss so that it became a sensual feast,

hot, hungry and fiercely possessive, escalating her excitement so that the pressure of his lips and the bold thrusts of
his tongue were not enough and she wanted more. His other
hand roamed up and down her body and cupped her bottom,
hauling her close so that she was made shockingly aware of
his powerful arousal pressing against her pelvis. She should
not be allowing him to do this, a warning voice whispered in
her head. But he dominated her senses, and a little shiver of
need ran through her when he slid his hand beneath the hem
of her tee shirt and skimmed his palm over her flat stomach,
the sensation of his fingertips stroking her bare flesh intensi-
fying the hot, throbbing ache between her legs.

His hand continued its determined journey upwards. Any
second now he would discover that she wasn't wearing a bra.
His questing fingers brushed the underside of her breast and
Ella snatched a sharp breath, lost to everything but her longing
for him to touch her where she had never permitted any man
to touch her before, to curve his hand around the small, firm
mound and caress the swollen nipple at its centre.

But, to her shock and scalding disappointment, he abruptly
ended the kiss. 'We need to leave soon, or we'll lose the restaurant booking,' he murmured coolly as he dropped his hand and
stepped away from her. 'You've got five minutes to get changed.'

Ella stared at him dazedly, her heart-rate gradually slowing
as shame at her wanton response to him replaced the frantic
drumbeat of desire. How could she have been so weak-willed
and so stupid? she wondered bitterly. She had given Vadim
completely the wrong idea about her, and now he no doubt
believed he could buy her dinner in exchange for sex. For a
wild moment she debated locking herself in her bedroom
until he went away—but what if he refused to leave? He had
already demonstrated his determination to get his own way,
and she had a strong suspicion that in a battle of wills he

would emerge the victor. Besides, she would be safer with him in a busy restaurant, she reasoned as she marched, stiff-backed, into her room and flung open her wardrobe. She thought it unlikely that he would make a public spectacle by kissing her in front of the other diners, and hopefully over a meal she would be able to convince him that she was serious about not wanting to have an affair with him. But as she stared at her face in the mirror, saw her swollen, reddened lips and her glazed eyes with their enlarged pupils, she acknowledged that the difficulty was going to be convincing herself.

CHAPTER FOUR

UP UNTIL eighteen months ago, Ella's working wardrobe had consisted of elegant but unexciting black dresses which she wore for performances. But when Marcus Benning had become her publicist and taken over the marketing side of her career he had insisted that she should go for a sexier image, and had persuaded her to buy daring designer outfits in a variety of coloured silks and satins. Naturally shy, she had struggled with her new look, especially when she'd found herself the focus of male attention, but now she was grateful for the make-over that had included lessons on how to apply make-up for her publicity photo-shoots. A light foundation, grey eyeshadow to highlight the colour of her eyes and black mascara to emphasise her lashes created a mask to hide behind, and the addition of bright red gloss on her lips completed the illusion of an elegant, coolly self-confident woman who was more than capable of rejecting unwanted advances from any man.

Unfortunately it *was* just an illusion, Ella acknowledged as she stepped into a red silk cocktail dress with spaghetti straps and a skirt that was shorter than she remembered it being when she'd tried it on in the shop. She felt brittle with nerves, and the pulse beating erratically at the base of her throat was a giveaway sign of her tension, but after sweeping her hair up into a chignon and spraying perfume on her wrists she could not put off returning to the sitting room and Vadim any longer.

He was standing by the fireplace, studying the many photographs of her mother, but turned as she entered the room. The flare of heat in his eyes as he subjected her to a leisurely inspection rattled her shaky composure. 'You look stunning, but I get the feeling you're making some sort of statement,' he murmured sardonically.

His perception was uncomfortably close to the mark, and Ella flushed. 'You'd prefer me to wear a sack?' she demanded tightly.

'You would look beautiful whatever you wore.' He paused for a heartbeat before adding outrageously, 'And exquisite wearing nothing at all.' He had closed the gap between them and was standing too close for comfort, the scent of his after-shave—a subtle blend of citrus and sandalwood—teasing her senses. 'However, I'd like to make one improvement.' He moved before she could guess his intention, placed his thumb-pad over her lips and wiped off her lipstick. 'That's better. Your lips are infinitely more kissable when they're not covered in gunk.'

'You've got a damn nerve,' Ella breathed, trembling with anger. 'I'm afraid you'll have to go to dinner alone. I've suddenly lost my appetite.'

'That is a pity, because I'm ravenous.' His eyes glinted wickedly as he trailed them down from her elegant hairstyle to her red stiletto shoes. 'And I hate to eat on my own; it makes me irritable, which is bad for my digestion. Anyway, you have to have something for dinner, and there's nothing in your fridge apart from a yoghurt that's past its sell-by date—I noticed when I helped myself to a glass of water and pinched a couple of ice-cubes.' He took advantage of Ella's fulminating silence to drop a stinging kiss on her lips before he spun her round and, to her utter fury, tapped her lightly on her derriere. 'A word of warning, angel face: I can't abide women who sulk,' he murmured dulcetly. 'Shall we go?'

'You are the most arrogant, overbearing…' Cheeks the same shade of scarlet as her dress, Ella snatched up her stole and purse and swept through the door he'd opened for her, her steps faltering as she passed the vase of roses on the dresser. The last rays of evening sunshine slanting through the windows turned the petals blood-red, and their sensuous fragrance seemed to mock her, but good manners forced her to turn to him. 'Thank you for the roses,' she muttered stiltedly. 'They're beautiful.'

'My pleasure.'

How could he infuse two simple words with such a wealth of meaning? she wondered. Or was she badly overreacting? She guessed that most of the women he dated were skilled in the art of flirting, and happy to indulge in verbal foreplay. But she felt on edge, unsure of her ability to handle a man as self-assured as Vadim, and it didn't help that her lips were still tingling from that last unsatisfactorily brief kiss.

On the way to the restaurant she was relieved that he did not seem to want to talk, although his brooding silence did nothing to ease her tension, and she darted him a surprised glance when he activated the CD player and her latest recording of Mendelssohn violin concertos filled the car.

'I first heard you play a year ago,' he said quietly, 'and I was blown away by your incredible talent. Undoubtedly your career will go from strength to strength.'

Sales of the CD had been high—hundreds, if not thousands of people must have listened to her play—but as the haunting notes of Mendelssohn's exquisite composition trembled between them in the close confines of the car Ella once again felt as though she had revealed her deepest emotions to Vadim, and it made her feel acutely vulnerable.

She was glad when they arrived in Mayfair. Simpson-Brown was reputed to be one of the best restaurants in the capital, and bookings were taken months in advance, but when they walked into the elegant front bar Vadim was greeted by the *maître-d'* like a long-lost brother and they were immediately escorted to a table.

'Do you come here often?' Ella queried when they finally took their seats, after Vadim had paused several times on their journey across the restaurant to greet other diners who had eagerly sought to gain his attention. The clichéd line sounded horribly gauche, and she coloured and quickly stared down at her menu, irritated with herself for acting like a teenager on her first date. It didn't help that Vadim was so impossibly gorgeous. She had been aware of the speculative glances directed his way by several beautiful women as he had crossed the restaurant. But his magnetism was due to more than the perfection of his sculpted features and the inherent strength of his lean, hard body. He possessed a raw, primitive quality which, laced with unquestionable power and more than a hint of danger, made him utterly irresistible to just about every female between the ages of sixteen and sixty.

He shrugged. 'I dine here maybe two or three times a month. I don't yet have a permanent base in London, so I've been living at a hotel in Bloomsbury for the past six months.' He paused fractionally and gave her an enigmatic glance across the table. 'But that situation is about to change.'

'Will you be going back to Paris? I read somewhere that you have a home there.' Even better, maybe he was planning to return to his native Russia, she mused, wondering with a sharp stab of impatience why her stomach dipped at the thought.

'It's true I have an apartment on the Champs-Elysées, but

I intend to settle in London for the foreseeable future to pursue various…' again he paused for a heartbeat '…interests.'

Undoubtedly he meant *business* interests, Ella assured herself frantically. But she could not control the quickening of her heart rate at the blatant sexual hunger in his gaze, nor drag her eyes from his sensual mouth that had wreaked havoc on her composure earlier. Get a grip, she ordered herself angrily. She was twenty-four years old, she had a successful career, and this was not the first time she'd been invited to dinner with a good-looking man—although it *was* the first time in her life she had been so intensely aware of a member of the opposite sex, she acknowledged ruefully.

The arrival of a waiter at their table to enquire whether they would like cocktails before they ate broke the tangible tension. 'I'll have a vodka martini.' Vadim glanced at Ella. 'We'll decide on red or white wine when we order dinner, but would you like an aperitif? Anton, here, can recommend several non-alcoholic cocktails if you prefer.'

Did he think she was so unsophisticated that she couldn't handle alcohol? Ella thought irritably. She gave him a cool smile and racked her brains for the name of a cocktail—any cocktail—that she'd heard of. 'I'd like a Singapore Sling, please.'

His dark brows lifted. 'Are you sure? The combination of gin and cherry brandy can be lethal on an empty stomach.'

In a minute he'd be ordering her a milkshake! 'I'll be fine, thank you,' she assured him coldly. The waiter left them, and she glanced around the packed restaurant, conscious that for the next hour or so she faced the unsettling prospect of talking exclusively to Vadim. Her nerves felt as taut as an over-stretched elastic band as she cast around for something to say, and she was relieved when the waiter reappeared almost instantly with their drinks.

Vadim lifted his glass. 'To new friendships…and new experiences,' he drawled, amusement glinting in his eyes when Ella took a cautious sip of her drink and made a choking sound which she hastily turned into a cough. Once again he was struck by her air of innocence, but in his experience all women were game-players, and no doubt Ella had her own agenda for acting the ingénue. He relaxed back in his seat and studied the menu, but to his irritation he could not prevent his gaze from straying across the table to absorb the delicate beauty of her face, the fragile line of her collarbone and the gentle curve of her pale breasts above her red dress. She was very lovely, and she had invaded his thoughts far too often recently, he mused as the dull ache in his groin intensified to a hot, throbbing sensation that caused him to shift uncomfortably in his chair.

'As a Russian who appreciates good caviar, I can recommend the Royal Beluga to start,' he murmured. 'And for the main, grilled Dover sole with Béarnaise sauce, or the grilled *poussin* with thyme and lemongrass are both excellent.'

Ella gave up struggling to understand the exotic menu, which featured among other things veal with a wasabi sorbet, and calf's liver with truffle mash. She could at least recognise caviar, although she had never tasted it, and she loved Dover sole. 'The caviar sounds fine, and I'd like the sole to follow, please.'

'I'll have the same.' Vadim gave their order to the waiter. 'And a bottle of Chablis, thank you.'

The waiter walked away, and, needing something to do with her hands, Ella lifted her glass and took another sip of her innocuous-looking red cocktail. It was rather too sweet for her liking, and tasted similar to cough linctus, but the alcoholic punch didn't seem so strong now that she was used to it. Aware that Vadim was watching her, she gave him a cool smile and took another sip.

'So, how old were you when you discovered your musical talent?' he queried.

'My mother gave me my first violin when I was four, but I was picking out tunes on the piano from as soon as I could climb up onto the piano stool.' Ella smiled softly. 'My earliest memories are of hearing my mother play. She was a truly remarkable musician, and I feel very privileged to have inherited a little of her talent.'

'Do you have any brothers or sisters?'

'No.' Ella paused. 'Mama developed a serious heart condition soon after I was born, which meant that she couldn't have any more children. We were very close,' she revealed huskily. 'Music created a special bond between us.'

Vadim gave her an intent look. 'I believe you said you were a teenager when she died? It must have been hard to deal with such a tragedy when you were so young.'

After more than a decade Ella still wasn't sure she had come to terms with the death of the person she had loved most in the world, but the conversation was straying into an area of her life she never discussed with anyone, so she gave a noncommittal shrug. 'It's in the past now. And at least I've been able to follow Mama's dream. She never had the opportunity to perform.' Ella's voice hardened. 'Especially once she married my father. But she always hoped I would have a successful career as a violinist. Before she died she set up a trust fund and left instructions for my musical education,' she explained to Vadim. 'Thanks to my mother I've studied under some of the best violin tutors in the world.'

'And do you enjoy performing? Was your mother's dream also your dream?' Vadim asked softly.

Ella frowned at him. 'Of course it was…is. What a strange question. Music is my life and I love playing.'

'That's not what I asked.' Vadim shrugged. 'It sounds a

little as though your life has been dictated by your mother from beyond the grave. I merely wondered whether you had ever considered a different career, or whether you truly have a burning ambition to be a successful soloist.'

'My life is not dictated by my dead mother,' Ella denied furiously. 'She just wanted me to have the chances that she never had, and I'm glad I've been able to fulfil her dream.' A solo career *was* her dream too, she assured herself, trying to ignore the voice in her head which pointed out that, although she loved playing as part of an orchestra, she did not enjoy the mind-numbing stage fright she suffered as a soloist. As for ever considering a different career—it was true she had briefly considered studying law, after she had been inspired by a talk at school given by a human rights lawyer. But she had quickly dismissed the idea. Music was her life, and she felt honour bound to follow the path her mother had planned for her.

'Mama hoped I would have a successful career so that I would be financially independent and never have to be reliant on a man, as she was on my father,' she said quietly. 'Music has given me that independence, and I regard that as my mother's greatest legacy.'

It was the second time she had intimated that she had issues regarding her father, and although Vadim never took an interest in the personal lives of the women he dated, he couldn't deny he was curious to learn more about Ella.

'After your mother died, I assume your father brought you up? Did you have a close relationship with him?'

For a second Ella pictured her father's cold, thin-lipped face, and the expression of undisguised dislike in his eyes on the few occasions when they had met. He had known that she'd hated him, and with his warped sense of humour and cruel tongue had found it amusing to taunt and provoke her, aware that her fear of him prevented her from voicing her feelings about him.

She suddenly became aware that Vadim was waiting for her to reply. 'No.' The single word snapped like a gunshot, and, seeing his surprise, she added hastily, 'I was away at boarding school, and he preferred to live in his villa in the South of France rather than at Stafford Hall, so I didn't see him very often.'

She could tell that Vadim wanted to ask more, but to her relief the waiter reappeared at their table with the first course. The caviar was heaped in a crystal bowl, which was set in a larger bowl filled with crushed ice, and as Ella stared at the small, shiny, black fish eggs, her appetite vanished.

'Um…this looks delicious,' she mumbled when the waiter set a plate of small buckwheat pancakes in front of her.

Vadim hid his smile. 'Have you actually eaten caviar before?'

Honesty seemed the best policy. 'No,' she admitted ruefully. 'I've heard it's an acquired taste.'

'It's the food of the gods,' he assured her. 'The proper Russian way of eating it is straight off the spoon, accompanied by a shot of frozen vodka. But, seeing as you are a caviar virgin, I think we'd better forget the vodka so that you can experience the ultimate pleasure of the taste and texture in your mouth.'

Ella felt her face flood with colour, and she wondered if Vadim had guessed that her virginity did not only encompass eating caviar. She watched him scoop a few of the shiny black eggs onto a glass spoon, and her eyes widened when he leaned across the table and held the spoon inches from her lips.

'Close your eyes and open your mouth,' he ordered, his deep, accented voice as sensuous as crushed velvet. His brilliant blue eyes burned into hers, and the atmosphere between them was suddenly charged with electricity as the restaurant, the other diners and the hubbub of voices all faded and there was only Vadim.

Utterly transfixed, Ella obediently lowered her lashes and felt the cold edge of the spoon against her lips, followed by the curious texture of smooth, round berries on her tongue. The taste was indescribable: slightly fishy, slightly salty and overwhelmingly rich, she noted, as her taste buds were seduced by the intensity of flavour. Her eyes flew open and locked with Vadim's piercing gaze. He was watching her reaction intently, and the whole experience was so incredibly sensual that Ella could not restrain the little shiver that ran down her spine.

'What is your verdict?'

She swallowed the last morsel of caviar and touched her tongue to her lips to catch the lingering taste, the unconscious action causing heat to burn in Vadim's groin. 'Heavenly,' she murmured huskily.

He inhaled sharply and forced himself to sit back in his seat, shattering the sexual tension that had held them both in its grip. 'Then eat,' he invited. 'Top a blini with sour cream, add a little of the caviar, and enjoy.'

As Ella followed his instructions she was shocked to find that her hands were shaking. For a moment there she had been completely bewitched by Vadim, and in all honesty she knew she would have been powerless to stop him if he had walked around the table, pulled her into his arms and made love to her right there in the middle of the crowded restaurant. Panic surged up inside her and she suddenly longed for the evening to be over. Vadim was too much. He overwhelmed her and made her feel things she had never felt before. Her body felt taut, each of her nerve-endings acutely sensitive, and when she glanced down she was horrified to see that her nipples were jutting provocatively against her red silk dress.

She shot him a furtive glance, and swallowed when she discovered that he was watching her, his eyes gleaming beneath his hooded lids before he deliberately dropped his gaze to her breasts. 'Do you go back to Russia often?' she asked him, in a desperate attempt to break the sensual spell he had woven around her.

'I own a house on the outskirts of Moscow, but I only go back once or twice a year now that most of my business interests are in Europe.'

'What about your family? Do they still live in Russia?'

For a second something flared in Vadim's eyes—a look of such raw pain that Ella almost gasped out loud. But then his lashes swept down and hid his expression, and when he met her gaze across the table his face was a handsome, unreadable mask. 'I have no family,' he said bluntly. 'Both my father and my grandmother, who helped to bring me up, died many years ago.'

Still shaken by the look she had glimpsed in his eyes, Ella took a sip of her wine, feeling instinctively that the loss of his father and grandmother had not been responsible for the savage emotion that had flared in his brilliant blue depths.

'What about your mother?'

He shrugged. 'She left when I was seven or eight. My father was a dour man, who spent most of his time at work or busy with his duties as a communist party official. As far as I know, my mother was much younger than him. I vaguely remember her smiling occasionally, which my father and grandmother never did, and I assume she wanted a better life than the one she had.'

'But she left you behind,' Ella murmured. She stared at Vadim's hard-boned face and felt something tug on her heart as she pictured him as a lonely little boy who had been abandoned by his mother. 'Was your grandmother kind?' What a ridiculous question, she berated herself impatiently, but for some reason his answer mattered. 'I mean…did she take good care of you?'

He gave a sardonic smile. 'My grandmother came from a

remote village in Siberia, where winter temperatures regularly drop to minus thirty degrees centigrade, and she was as tough as the climate she grew up in. She was in her seventies when I was born, and I doubt she welcomed having to take on the role of parent in her old age. She certainly never seemed to find any pleasure in my presence, and despite her elderly years she had a heavy hand with the belt—until I learned to run fast enough to escape her, when she passed the duty of beating me over to my father,' he said, in a voice devoid of any emotion.

'That's horrible,' Ella said, paling. 'It sounds like you had a tough childhood.'

Vadim thought briefly of the relentless greyness of his early years, and gave another shrug. 'I survived. And compared with the two years I spent in the army my boyhood was a picnic.'

He said no more, but his silence was somehow more evocative than words. Ella recalled a newspaper article she had once read about the institutional violence and bullying that was regularly meted out to young recruits in the Russian army, and she guessed that Vadim had learned to be physically and mentally tough to cope. She tore her gaze from him and forced herself to eat her dinner. The Dover sole was delicious, but her appetite had disappeared. She could not forget the flash of pain in his eyes when she had first asked about his family, and she couldn't help feeling that there were secrets in his past he had not revealed.

'Have you ever tried to trace your mother? I mean, she might still be alive.'

Vadim ate the last of his fish and took a long sip of his wine. 'Very possibly, but I have no interest in her. Why would I?' he demanded coolly. 'She walked away when I needed her most, and I learned from the experience never to put my faith in another human being.'

He had clearly been more affected by his mother leaving

than he admitted, perhaps even to himself, Ella brooded. She knew from experience that the emotional scars from an unhappy childhood still hurt long into adulthood, and now she had a better understanding of why he had earned a reputation as a womaniser who refused to commit to any of his lovers.

She and Vadim shared a common bond in that they had both been affected by their upbringing, she realised. Having witnessed the misery her mother had endured at the hands of her father, she was not looking for commitment, and certainly not for marriage. She valued her independence as much as Vadim did—but could she have a no-strings affair with him, as he had suggested, and emerge with her heart unscathed? Her instincts warned her that she would be playing with fire, but the feral gleam in his eyes stirred a feeling of wild reck-lessness within her and a longing to experience the hungry passion he promised.

She darted a glance across the table and discovered that he was watching her with a brooding intensity she found unnerv-ing. In an effort to lighten the curiously tense atmosphere that had fallen between them she gave him a tentative smile.

Why did Ella's smile remind him of Irina? Vadim asked himself savagely. With her pale blonde hair and English rose colouring she bore no resemblance to his wife, who had been olive-skinned, like him, and had had thick, dark brown hair. But the two women shared the same smile. He closed his eyes briefly, as if he could somehow blot out the pain that surged through him. Irina's face swam before him, and her gentle, hopeful smile tore at his heart. She had been a quiet, shy young woman, as gentle as a doe with her soft brown eyes. She hadn't asked for much from life, he acknowledged grimly—just that he should love her. And he had, Vadim assured himself. He *had* loved Irina—but to his lasting regret he had not appreciated how much she had meant to him until he had held her limp, cold body in his arms.

Ella's smile faded when Vadim's hard expression did not lighten, and her stomach lurched with a mixture of embarrassment and disappointment when he continued to stare at her meditatively. She had the impression that although he was looking at her he did not see her, and she wondered where his thoughts had taken him.

To her relief the waiter arrived, to enquire whether they wanted dessert. Vadim suddenly jerked back to the present, his mouth curving into a sensual smile that made her heart race, and to her chagrin she could not prevent herself from smiling back at him. When he turned on the charm he was utterly irresistible, she thought ruefully. She knew it would be very easy to fall for him, but he was a far more complex man than his playboy persona revealed, and her instincts warned her to guard her emotions against him.

Vadim steered the conversation onto other topics for the rest of the meal. He was an entertaining and intelligent companion, with a dry wit that frequently made Ella smile, and over the delectable bitter chocolate mousse she chose for dessert she found herself falling ever deeper under his spell. He could charm the birds from the trees, she thought ruefully. But the few scant facts he had revealed about himself over the course of the evening she could have discovered on the Internet, and she wondered if he ever permitted anyone to see the real Vadim Aleksandrov. He possessed an inherent dangerous quality that both repelled and intrigued her, but although she reminded herself that he was a heartless playboy, like her father had been, she sensed an unexpected vulnerability about him that made her wish she could learn more about the man behind the mask.

'So, what are your plans for your career?' he asked her over coffee. Although he had revealed little about himself, he had encouraged her to talk about her life as a musician, and her years studying at the Royal College of Music, and somehow he had drawn her into telling him personal confidences that she only ever shared with a few close friends.

After her cocktail and two glasses of wine Ella was feeling pleasantly relaxed, and filled with an uncharacteristic boldness which had led her to discover that flirting was fun—particularly with a man as wickedly sexy as Vadim.

'I'm giving a solo performance at the Palais Garnier in Paris next week, and after that I'll mainly be in London, to record the soundtrack for a film and work on my next solo album.'

His slow smile stole her breath, and the heat in his eyes caused a peculiar dragging sensation deep in her pelvis. 'It so happens that I will also be based mainly in London for the next couple of months, which presents us with an ideal opportunity to get to know one another better,' he said with undisguised satisfaction.

His vivid blue eyes lingered on her mouth, before trailing a leisurely path over her slim shoulders and down to her breasts, leaving Ella in no doubt as to how he hoped to get acquainted with her body. Her new-found confidence trickled away, and she said hurriedly, 'I'm going to be working incredibly hard, and I really won't have time for anything else…'

He leaned across the table and stopped her flow of words by placing his finger across her lips. Her eyes flew to his, her unguarded expression of fearful anticipation causing Vadim to once again question his motives. There was a sweetness and a curious naïveté about her that reminded him of Irina, and for a moment his conscience nagged that it would be unfair to instigate an affair when he was certain he would tire of her within a matter of weeks. He would not want to get her hopes up that she could ever be more to him than a fleeting sexual encounter. But her lips felt soft and moist against his skin, and the temptation to replace his finger with his mouth and kiss her into submission caused his body to harden. Fantasies about making love to her had dominated his thoughts from the moment he had met her, and the only solution, he decided grimly, was to sleep with her until he'd got her out of his system.

'You know what they say about all work and no play,' he drawled softly. 'We could have fun together, angel face.'

Maybe he was right, Ella debated silently while he settled the bill. An affair with Vadim would undoubtedly be fun while it lasted, and, contrary to her friend Jenny's belief, she did not want to live like a nun for the rest of her life. She might be inexperienced, her knowledge of sex gleaned from movies and popular women's magazines, but she knew enough to be confident that Vadim would be an inventive and uninhibited lover, who would arouse her to a fever-pitch of desire and appease the aching need he evoked.

The London streets were buzzing when they left the restaurant, the pavements crowded with people and the roads jammed with traffic, car headlights and street-lights illuminating the night sky. Vadim slid a protective arm around Ella's waist as she was jostled by a group of young men who had piled out of a bar. 'Do you want me to take you home, or would you like to go on to a club?'

His hard body was pressed against hers, making her acutely aware of the muscular strength of his thighs, and she could feel the heat that emanated from him and smell the intoxicating scent of his cologne mingled with another perfume that was innately male. Her common sense insisted that she should ask him to take her home, where she would bid him a polite goodnight and make it clear that she did not want to see him again. But for the first time in her life she felt like rebelling against the constraints of her life, which suddenly seemed to be one long round of practising and performing, leaving her little opportunity to socialise. She usually went to bed after the ten o'clock news—but she was twenty-four, for heaven's sake, she reminded herself impatiently, and it was time she lived a little.

'A club might be fun,' she murmured, and was rewarded with a sensual smile that sent a quiver of awareness down her spine.

'I'm a member of Annabel's in Berkeley Square. It's not far from here. Are you happy to walk?' As he spoke, Vadim curled his big hand around her smaller one, the faint abrasion of his skin against the softness of her palm so incredibly sensual that Ella simply nodded and fell into step beside him, her heart thudding in time with the tap of her stiletto heels on the pavement.

CHAPTER FIVE

ANNABEL'S nightclub was a popular haunt of the rich and famous, and Ella spotted numerous celebrities on the dance floor, but she noticed that guests and staff alike seemed slightly in awe of Vadim. Once again she was aware of his power and his magnetic attraction, which drew beautiful women to him in droves. He could take his pick from any of the number of models and socialites in the bar, many of whom brazenly tried to catch his attention. They were uniformly exquisite, with long, tanned limbs, perfect figures and flawless features, and Ella couldn't help comparing herself with them and wondering why on earth he was interested in her.

But Vadim seemed to only have eyes for her. She could not help but find his attention flattering, and as the night progressed and the champagne flowed she began to relax and enjoy herself. Dancing to the funky club classics was fun, and dancing with Vadim, held close against his chest while he moved his pelvis sinuously against hers, sent molten heat coursing through her veins.

'Enjoying yourself?' he drawled, his blue eyes gleaming as he glanced down at her flushed face. The music had slowed and they were drifting around the dance floor, hip to hip, while his hand strayed up and down her spine in a sensuous caress.

'Yes,' Ella admitted honestly. There seemed no point in denying it when she felt more alive and exhilarated than she could ever remember feeling.

'Good.' Vadim lowered his head slowly towards her, and she could not restrain a little shiver of excitement when he slanted his mouth over hers and initiated a slow, drugging kiss. His lips were firm, demanding her response, and she gave it helplessly, her whole body trembling when he slid his tongue into her mouth and explored her moist warmth with devastating efficiency until she sagged against him, so lost in this new world of sensory pleasure that the people around them on the dance floor faded, and there was no one but Vadim.

It was three a.m. when they finally left the club, and as they stepped outside the blast of fresh air made Ella's head spin.

'This isn't your car,' she mumbled, when a sleek black limousine pulled up next to them and its chauffeur sprang out to open the rear door.

'I never drive after I've had a couple of drinks. I arranged for my driver to take the Aston Martin back to my hotel and come back to collect us in the limo.' Vadim frowned as he watched Ella wobble precariously on her high heels. 'Are you okay?'

'Of course I'm okay. Why shouldn't I be?' She bent to climb into the car, misjudged the height of the door fame and winced as she hit her head. 'I've never felt better,' she assured him brightly. It was true; several glasses of champagne had replaced her usual reserve with brimming confidence, and she felt sexy and uninhibited and desperate for Vadim to kiss her again. She stared at him hopefully and instinctively traced her lips with the tip of her tongue, anticipation shivering through her when his eyes narrowed and gleamed with feral hunger.

But it was warm in the car, and the smooth motion of the engine had a soporific effect on her, so that her eyelids felt heavy and her head drooped onto Vadim's shoulder. She looked about sixteen, he brooded impatiently. Tendrils of hair had escaped her chignon, and he carefully released the clip on top of her head so that the silky mass tumbled around her shoulders.

The type of woman he usually dated would have spent the journey home stroking her hand over his thigh as a prelude to a night of mutually satisfying sex—not snuggling up to him like a sleepy kitten. There was something about Ella that tugged at his conscience, and not for the first time he wondered if he had made a mistake by pursuing her—especially since he had discovered that she carried a truckload of emotional baggage which seemed to be linked with her unhappy relationship with her father.

Emotions were complicated, which was why he did not deal in them. He had failed Irina and broken her heart, and he refused to ever be responsible for another woman's emotional security.

Ella frowned when the comfortable pillow beneath her neck moved, so that her head lolled unsupported. Someone gripped her shoulder and shook her, and an impatient voice sounded in her ear. 'Ella, wake up. We're back at Kingfisher House.'

Her heavy lids lifted and she stared into Vadim's startling blue eyes. His face was inches from hers, his mouth so tantalisingly close that she moistened her lips with the tip of her tongue in unconscious invitation.

Hot sexual excitement uncoiled in Vadim's gut, and for a few seconds he was tempted to ignore the nagging voice of his conscience, which warned that Ella seemed far more innocent than he had first thought. She was a consenting adult, and she wanted him, the voice in his head argued. Her grey eyes were smoky with desire, and her soft parted lips were just begging for him to possess them. But she'd had a couple of glasses of champagne on top of the wine and cocktails they had drunk with dinner, and he was sure she was not used to drinking alcohol. He had done many things in his past which he regretted, and he refused to add taking advantage of a naïve girl who reminded him too much of his dead wife to the list.

'Come on, I'll see you inside,' he said abruptly, when she scrambled inelegantly out of the car and stood beside him on the gravel drive, swaying slightly.

Ella gave a puzzled frown when Vadim took hold of her arm and marched her up to the house. A moment ago she had been sure that he was about to kiss her, and she had been surprised and disappointed when he had abruptly pulled back and leapt out of the car. Maybe he had been conscious of the presence of the chauffeur and wanted to be alone with her when he kissed her? She cast a sideways glance at his handsome face and a frisson of excitement tingled down her spine as she imagined him slanting his sensual mouth over hers. Would he stop at kissing, or was he intending to sweep her into his arms, carry her through to her bedroom and make love to her?

She fumbled in her bag for her key, opened the front door and turned back to face him, heart thudding painfully beneath her ribs. His sensual smile stole her breath, and she felt as taut as an overstrung bow as she waited for him to take her in his arms.

'Goodnight, Ella.'

Goodnight! She stared at him in confusion as he stepped back from her. When they had left the nightclub the hungry gleam in his eyes had convinced her that he wanted to take their relationship a step further. He intrigued her in a way no other man ever had, and on the journey back to Kingfisher House she had made the decision that she was ready to explore the sexual chemistry that simmered between them.

But Vadim was leaving! Perhaps he was waiting for a sign from her that she would not reject him if he kissed her? He had turned away from her and was walking towards his waiting car. Taking a deep breath, she blurted out, 'Would you like to come in…for coffee?'

He paused and slowly turned back to face her, his intent stare causing hot colour to stain her cheeks. Seconds ticked past, stretching her nerves, but then he gave a shrug and strolled back up the drive. The moonlight slanted across his face, throwing his sculpted features into sharp relief. He was so incredibly handsome, and so intensely male, Ella thought as she inhaled the exotic scent of his cologne mingled with the subtle perfume of pheromones that inflamed her senses. He rejoined her on the doorstep, and the heat emanating from his muscular body caused a curious melting sensation deep in her pelvis. She had never been so sexually aware of a man in her life, and acting purely on instinct she swayed towards him, lifted her face to his.

He muttered something in Russian, but Ella was too distracted by her longing to feel his mouth on hers to wonder what the words meant. Her heart slammed against her ribs when he lowered his dark head and brushed his lips over hers in a delicate tasting that left her quivering for more. Lost to everything but his sensual sorcery, she opened her mouth for him to deepen the kiss, and felt a jolt of pleasure when he slid his tongue deep into her moist warmth and initiated an intimate exploration that escalated her excitement to fever-pitch.

She could not resist him, nor the dictates of her body, which was eager to experience this new world of sensory pleasure. With a soft sigh she slid her arms up to his shoulders so that her breasts were pressed against his chest. She was impatient for him to curve his arms around her waist and draw her closer still, but to her utter shock he suddenly ended the kiss and caught hold of her hands to prevent her from linking them around his neck.

'Thanks for the invitation,' he drawled, 'but I have to get back.'

Still trembling with sexual anticipation, Ella could not

disguise her disappointment. 'But I thought…' She trailed to a halt and snatched her fingers out of his grasp, her cheeks burning when she realised that Vadim was not about to carry her into the house and seduce her. She had practically leapt on him, she thought sickly. She had instigated the kiss, and from his mocking smile he was clearly amused by her eagerness.

Something flared in his eyes when she jerked away from him. 'It's debatable who you're going to hate most tomorrow, angel face—yourself, or me,' he said gently. He turned and strode back to his car without a backward glance, and with a yelp of fury at her own stupidity Ella shot into the house and slammed the door behind her.

Ella opened her eyes to find bright sunshine streaming into her room, and when she glanced at the clock she was shocked to discover that it was almost midday. Her head felt woolly, but, like a theatre curtain slowly opening, the mist in her brain cleared and her memory returned with a vengeance. Last night she'd had dinner with Vadim and he had fed her caviar. Afterwards they had visited a club and danced until the early hours before he had brought her home, whereupon she had practically begged him to spend the night with her—and he had rejected her!

Utterly mortified, she rolled onto her stomach and dragged the pillow over her head. What had she been thinking? she asked herself furiously. But of course she *hadn't* been thinking—not properly—and her actions had been fuelled by too much champagne. That must have been the case—because why else would she have decided that she could handle an affair with Vadim, when she knew he was a playboy and the sort of man she usually avoided like the plague?

She would never be able to face him again, she thought miserably, her face burning with shame when she recalled how she had leaned close to him when they had stood on the doorstep, made it clear that she wanted him to kiss her. Had he found her eagerness off-putting? Maybe he had been playing a game, which he'd won once she had shown her willingness to sleep with him? The idea made her feel sick, and she hauled herself out of bed and staggered into her small kitchen to discover that she had run out of milk and teabags.

Several glasses of water and a shower later she felt marginally better—physically, at least. But the recriminations and self-disgust continued, and, desperate to get out of the house, she pulled on jeans and a tee shirt, flung open the French doors and stepped outside. The garden was a blaze of colour, the emerald lawn bordered by flowers in a variety of brilliant shades, but it was the sight of Vadim—sitting at the garden table further along the terrace—that stopped her in her tracks.

'What…what are you doing here?' she croaked, so taken aback by his appearance that she could barely articulate the words. Her shock at seeing him, after she had hoped that they would never meet again, had turned her legs to jelly, and she dropped weakly onto a chair opposite him. It didn't help that he looked utterly gorgeous, in sun-bleached jeans and a black polo shirt open at the throat to reveal a glimpse of bronzed skin overlaid with dark chest hair. Unlike her, he was clearly not suffering any adverse effects from the champagne they had drunk at the club last night, she noted darkly. He looked completely relaxed as he leisurely perused the Sunday papers, while the delicious aroma of freshly brewed coffee rose from the jug in front of him.

'Good afternoon,' he drawled, glancing pointedly at his watch. 'I take it you slept well.'

'I don't understand why—or how—you're here,' Ella muttered, wishing he would remove his designer shades so that she could see the expression in his eyes. A high-pitched voice drew her attention down the garden, and her surreal feeling intensified when she watched her cousin's young daughter, Lily, run across the lawn.

'Ella! We came to see you, but you were asleep,' the little girl greeted her. 'Grandpa said we'd better not wake you up.'

'Yes, I had a bit of a lie-in this morning,' Ella said weakly, flushing when she caught Vadim's amused glance. She hugged Lily. 'Is Grandpa here?'

'He's there.' Lily pointed, and Ella looked round to see her uncle Rex, walking across the lawn towards them.

'There you are, Ella.' Rex Portman studied his niece's pale face and chuckled. 'Been partying, have you? Good for you. I've always said you spend too much time locked away with your violin. Girls of your age should be out having fun.' His eyes moved from Ella to Vadim and back again, 'I take it you've introduced yourself? I phoned a couple of times earlier, to let you know Vadim was taking over the tenancy of Kingfisher House today, but you must have been out for the count. I don't suppose you even heard the delivery van arrive, or the army of staff Vadim hired to carry his things into the house—did you?'

'I…' Ella made a strangled sound and decided she had obviously been transported into the world of Alice in Wonderland. She wouldn't be surprised if an oversized white rabbit suddenly appeared and they all had a tea party.

'Don't look so worried,' her uncle said jovially. 'I've explained to Vadim that you currently live in the caretaker flat, and he's happy for the situation to continue—at least for the next couple of months.'

'Yes indeed.' Vadim's gravelly Russian accent was deep and melodious compared to Uncle Rex's chirpy, good-humoured voice. 'I frequently travel abroad for business, and it suits me that the house will not be completely empty while I'm away.'

His smile oozed charm, but for once Ella was immune to it and clenched her fists beneath the table. 'Until I decide whether or not to buy Kingfisher House I won't be employing any live-in staff, so you are welcome to remain in the staff accommodation,' he said smoothly. He paused, and then added softly, 'I understand you need to find a flat big enough to house a grand piano?'

'That piano's a liability, if you ask me,' Uncle Rex said before Ella could comment. 'Monstrous thing it is. You might have to think about selling it, Ella.'

She shook her head fiercely. 'Mama's piano is one of the few mementos I have of her. I'll never sell it.'

Her uncle grimaced. 'Well, thanks to Vadim's generosity, you won't have to for now.'

The words on Ella's tongue, which had been queuing up to tell Vadim in no uncertain terms what he could do with his offer for her to remain at Kingfisher House, juddered to a halt. Her eyes flew to his face, and she was certain that behind his concealing shades his eyes were glinting with satisfaction that he had her right where he wanted her. *Nothing* would induce her to sell her mother's piano, and even if she spent every spare moment searching for a flat it would be weeks before she found somewhere suitable, she acknowledged grimly.

'Grandpa, I want to see the water,' Lily piped up. She darted, quick as an eel, across the lawn, and Uncle Rex hurried after her.

'Hang on a minute. Don't you go too close to the river, young lady.'

Ella watched them go, and then turned angrily to Vadim. 'Is this your peculiar idea of a joke?' She snatched a breath and rushed on, without giving him a chance to reply. 'I can't believe you had the *gall* to engineer this.'

Dark brows rose quizzically. 'Engineer what, specifically?'

'You taking over the tenancy of Kingfisher House,' she said

fiercely. 'Don't tell me it wasn't planned. I suppose you decided to rent the house after you found out that I live here.'

'Actually, there was no Machiavellian plot,' he said mildly. 'I've known Rex Portman for some time, and my company has bought several properties with development potential through his estate agency. When he heard I was looking for a base in the UK he showed me around Kingfisher House, and I immediately decided to rent it for six months.' Okay, that was stretching the truth, Vadim conceded silently, but he saw no reason to admit to Ella that he had originally decided to move into a house in Belgravia, but had changed his mind the night he had driven her home after the concert at Amesbury House.

Ella blushed as she recalled how he had rejected her the previous night. Of course he had not plotted to share the house with her, she told herself impatiently. But during their dinner date she had been so sure that he desired her, and when they had danced together at Annabel's she had felt the hard proof of his arousal nudge insistently against her pelvis. Had she read the signs wrongly? Or had Vadim for some reason had a change of heart on the drive back to Kingfisher House and decided that he no longer wanted to explore the sexual chemistry between them? His face was shuttered, giving no clue to his thoughts. He was an enigma, and once again she had the feeling that there were secrets in his past she knew nothing about.

He finally took off his sunglasses, and the amused gleam in his brilliant blue eyes fuelled her temper. 'You must see the situation is impossible,' she said bitterly. 'I can't live here with you.'

Vadim leaned back in his chair and studied her broodingly. 'We won't technically be living together,' he murmured laconically.

She glared at him, her pride still smarting. 'You're right— we won't,' she said sharply. 'The staff flat has its own separate entrance, and the door between the flat and the main house will be locked at all times.'

She knew from the way his eyes narrowed that she had angered him, but his voice was level when he spoke. 'What do you think I'm going to do—barge my way into your room and force myself on you? I have never taken a woman against her will in my life,' he assured her coldly. 'You have nothing to fear from me, Ella. But may I remind you that yesterday you made it clear that you hoped I would spend the night with you.'

Scarlet with embarrassment, Ella was forced to bite back her angry retort when Lily dashed back up the garden and threw herself onto her lap. 'Mummy's had a new baby,' the little girl announced.

'I know. His name's Tom, isn't it?' Ella ruffled her goddaughter's curls and thought briefly of her cousin Stephanie, who had given birth to her second child three days ago. 'Is he tiny?'

Lily nodded and held up her doll. 'I've got a new baby too. Her name's Tracy.' She paused, her attention drawn to the big, dark-haired man sitting opposite. 'What's your name?'

'Vadim,' he replied, his smile deepening when the little girl frowned.

'You sound funny.'

Ella shot him a lightning glance, but to her surprise Vadim appeared quite at ease talking to a young child.

'That's because I come from another country,' he explained, in the gravelly accent that brought Ella's skin out in goose bumps. 'I am from Russia.'

Lily's eyes were as round as saucers as she regarded Vadim for several seconds before nodding her approval. 'You can hold Tracy if you like.'

'Thank you.' Vadim stared down at the rag-doll Lily had placed on the table in front of him, and closed his eyes briefly as pain swept through him. It was incredible how after all this time the sight of a doll could open up the floodgate of memories. His mind flew back across the years and he saw another doll, another little girl.

'*You hold my dolly, Papa. Sacha's scared on the swing.*' He could hear Klara's sweet, childish voice, speaking in Russian, as clearly as if she had just uttered the words. '*Promise you'll take care of her, Papa?*'

'*Of course I will, devochka moya. I'll take care of both of you.*'

But he had broken his promise, Vadim thought grimly, pain slicing his insides like a knife in his gut. He hadn't taken care of his little daughter, nor her mother. He picked up Lily's beautifully dressed doll, with its bright golden curls, and thought of the raggedy doll with brown wool hair that Irina had so painstakingly mended each time the stitching had broken and more stuffing had spilled out.

'*When the business does better I'll buy Klara a new doll,*' he had told Irina as she'd squinted to thread her needle in their poorly lit apartment.

'*She likes this one.*' Irina had stared at him, her pretty face troubled. '*And she'd rather see her papa more often than have a new doll.*'

It was a pity he hadn't listened. The guilt would be with him for ever.

'Do you like Tracy?' Lily's voice wrenched him back to the present. 'I got her for my birthday.'

'She's a beautiful doll,' he assured her gravely. 'How old were you on your birthday, Lily?'

'Five.'

The knife sliced again, deeper; the pain no longer the dull ache that served as a constant reminder of the past but so agonisingly sharp that he inhaled swiftly. Klara had been just five years old. It was no time at all, he brooded dully. She should have had so much longer on this earth, but instead she had been buried by the tons of snow that had hurtled down the mountainside and all but wiped out Irina's home village.

Ten years had passed since that fateful day when his wife and little daughter had been killed by an avalanche, and he had learned to contain his grief. But Lily, with her cheeky smile and halo of curls, was an agonising reminder of all he had lost. And the limp rag-doll, which travelled with him wherever he went in the world, was a poignant link with the only two people he had ever loved.

CHAPTER SIX

'WELL, Vadim, I think we'd better give you some peace to settle into Kingfisher House,' Rex Portman gasped, panting and pink-faced from chasing his granddaughter around the garden. 'There's not much else to show you, apart from the summerhouse down by the river. If there's anything else you need to know, Ella will be able to help. She's lived here for—what is it now, Ella—four years? She was responsible for most of the interior decoration too. I'm sure you'll admit she's done a classy job.'

'The house is delightful,' Vadim murmured, replacing his sunglasses on his nose so that his expression was unreadable. The demons that haunted him were too private and personal to be shared, and he had never spoken of his past to anyone.

'Oh, I almost forgot. Photos of the new baby.' Rex extracted a packet of photographs from his pocket and handed them to Ella. 'Handsome little chap, isn't he? Steph says he looks a lot like me.'

Ella stared at the round red face and bald head of her cousin's newborn baby son, glanced at her uncle's sweat-beaded pate, and conceded that there was a strong resemblance.

'He's very sweet,' she said softly, surprised by the pang of maternal longing that gripped her.

Uncle Rex nodded. 'I expect you'll want to settle down and have a couple of kids of your own soon.'

She shook her head firmly. 'I doubt I'll ever have children. For one thing, I believe children should grow up with two parents who are committed to each other,' she explained, when her uncle gave her an incredulous look, 'and as I never want to get married I'm just going to have to enjoy being a godmother.' She gave Lily a hug, and was rewarded when the little girl squeezed her so hard that her ribs felt in danger of cracking. It wasn't that she did not like children, she mused. She adored Lily, and loved spending time with her, but music and her career put huge demands on her time and she had always thought it would be selfish to have a child when she spent five or six hours a day playing.

'Well, there's plenty of time for you to meet a chap and change your mind,' Uncle Rex assured her cheerfully, patently believing she needed reassurance that she wouldn't end up a childless spinster. But she wouldn't change her mind, she thought fiercely. She accepted that not all marriages were the route to hell—Rex and her mother's sister, Aunt Lorna, had been happily married for thirty years—but they were the exception rather than the norm. Many of her friends had divorced parents and split families, and she would never put herself or a child through all that misery.

But if she was certain she did not want to get married, what *did* she want? Ella brooded later that afternoon, asking herself the same question that Jenny had posed when Vadim had sent her the bouquet of red roses. Until now music had dominated her life and she hadn't given men or relationships much thought. But all that had changed when she had met Vadim in Paris. Since then he had invaded her mind far too often, and when he kissed her and touched her… She bit her lip and tried to dismiss the erotic fantasy of their naked bodies intimately entwined.

Suddenly her life, which had been plodding along quite nicely, was in turmoil, and she no longer knew what she wanted. She could not remain at Kingfisher House when Vadim would be an unnervingly close neighbour, but she had no choice until she found another flat, she debated with herself. There was only one way to deal with the confused thoughts in her head, and that was to lose herself in music. Her violin was a faithful friend, and a sense of calm settled over her when she settled her chin on the chin-rest and drew her bow across the strings.

For the next hour or two there was no danger that she would disturb the new tenant of Kingfisher House. Shortly after Uncle Rex and Lily had left Vadim had announced that he was going to a nearby pub for lunch. She had turned down his invitation to join him, citing the need to get on with some household chores. She would spend an hour running through the piece by Debussy that she hoped to include on her next album, and after that she would no longer be able to put off visiting the supermarket to restock her fridge.

'Do you realise you've been playing virtually without a break for three hours?' Vadim's deep voice came from the French doors, which Ella had left open. 'Maybe longer,' he added. He had arrived back at the house after lunch to hear the strains of Elgar drifting across the garden, and instead of a reading an important financial report, as he had planned, he'd spent the afternoon listening to Ella play. 'It's time to come and eat,' he told her, when she lowered her violin and frowned at him.

'Eat?' she said vaguely. 'What's the time?'

'Almost seven.'

'Damn!' Ella came back to reality with a thump. The supermarket shut at four on Sundays, her fridge was a barren wilderness, and the growl from her stomach reminded her that she hadn't eaten all day. A delicious smell was drifting in from the terrace. She sniffed appreciatively and Vadim's lips twitched.

'I ordered dinner. Do you like Thai food?'

Hunger battled with the decision she'd made earlier that, for the few weeks until she found another flat, she and Vadim would lead completely separate lives. Hunger won. 'I love it.'

'Good.' His brief smile broke the stern lines of his face, but she noticed that it did not reach his eyes. He seemed remote, almost sombre tonight, and for a moment she sensed an inner loneliness about him that tugged on her heart. It was gone before she could define what she had seen. His mask slipped back into place and his smile widened seductively, causing her heart to flip in her chest. 'Come through when you're ready,' he invited, and disappeared back to his part of the house.

There was no reason why she should not eat with him dressed as she was, Ella acknowledged, glancing down at her jeans. But the sultry June evening provided a perfect excuse to change into the delicate silvery-grey silk dress she'd bought recently, after Jenny had persuaded her that it brought out the colour of her eyes. It took mere seconds to darken her lashes with mascara and apply a pale pink gloss to her lips, and she left her hair loose, sprayed Chanel to her pulse-points and swiftly appraised her reflection in the mirror, dismayed to find that the eyes staring back at her were as dark as woodsmoke, and her cheeks were flushed with the rosy glow of unbidden excitement.

It was just dinner, she reminded herself when she slipped out of the French doors and walked a few steps along the terrace to the second set of doors leading into the main house. Tonight she would be on her guard against Vadim's seductive charm. She paused in the doorway, her eyes drawn to the table set for two, the tall candles in elegant silver holders casting soft light over the centrepiece of white roses. It was intimate, romantic… Ella swiftly dismissed the idea. Vadim was not interested in romance. She had thought that he wanted to sleep with her, but now she wasn't sure about that—any more than she was sure about what she wanted, she admitted to herself ruefully. But when he walked towards her, looking devastatingly sexy in close-fitting black trousers and a fine white silk shirt through which she could see the shadow of dark body hair, her heart set up a slow, thudding beat, and she could almost touch the searing sexual electricity that quivered in the air between them.

'You look beautiful,' he greeted her quietly. Three simple words, but the slight roughness of his voice turned the compliment into a sensual caress that made the tiny hairs on her skin stand on end, and the gleam beneath his heavy lids evoked a slow-burning fire deep in her pelvis.

'Thank you.' Did that breathless, *sexy* voice really belong to her? When he drew out a chair she sat down thankfully, and took her time unfolding her napkin while she fought for composure.

'Would you like champagne?' Vadim lifted a bottle of Krug from the ice bucket, but Ella shook her head and quickly filled her glass with water from the jug on the table.

'Water will be fine, thanks,' she murmured, blushing at his mocking smile that told her he understood her determination to keep a clear head this evening. He trapped her gaze and she found it impossible to look away, the tension between them almost tangible until suddenly, shockingly, a figure walked into the room and the sensual spell was broken.

'Ah—dinner,' Vadim announced, walking around the table to take his place opposite her. 'Tak-Sin is one of the best Thai chefs in London. I hope you're hungry,' he added, when the man pushed a trolley laden with a variety of dishes over to the table.

'When you said you'd ordered dinner, I assumed it would be delivered in plastic cartons,' Ella murmured wryly, her taste buds stirring as Tak-Sin placed a bowl of clear, fragrant soup in front of her. She smiled at the chef, who promptly reeled off the names of the dishes he was placing on the table.

'Gai phadd prek, goong preaw wann…'

'He doesn't speak much English,' Vadim explained, when she looked at him helplessly. 'The first dish is chicken with green peppers, and that one is prawns with sweet and sour vegetables. This is some sort of beef dish—I think…'

'Well, it looks and smells gorgeous, so I guess the names don't matter,' Ella said as she picked up her spoon and tasted the soup. The food was nectar to her empty stomach, and she spent the next ten minutes sampling each of the dishes with such concentration that Vadim smiled.

'I'm glad to see you enjoy your food. Most of the women I know seem to survive by nibbling on lettuce leaves and the occasional breadstick.'

'I guess I'm lucky that I can eat what I like and never gain weight,' Ella said with a shrug. 'But the downside is that I'll probably always be scrawny and flat-chested.'

'I would describe you as slender, rather than scrawny.' Vadim paused and trailed his eyes over her slim shoulders and the delicate upper slopes of her breasts revealed above the neckline of her dress. 'And although your breasts are small they suit your tiny frame. I think it's a pity that so many young women have breast implants and end up looking as though they've stuffed a couple of footballs under their clothes. I definitely prefer the natural look,' he added softly, his eyes gleaming wickedly when Ella blushed.

Trying not to dwell on the hordes of women he had dated in the past, and desperate to steer the conversation away from the size of her breasts, she seized on the first thing that came into her head. 'I believe your company is the biggest mobile phone company in Russia, and now has a major stake in the European market? How did you start out selling phones?'

'I actually started out selling Russian dolls. Yes, really.' Vadim laughed when Ella looked at him disbelievingly. 'Matryoshka dolls—you've probably seen them; they're made of wood, usually about seven in a set, and they fit one inside another from the smallest to the biggest. When I left the army the political situation in Russia was changing, and in the early days of post-communism it was possible for the first time to set up a private business.' He paused to take a sip of champagne before continuing. 'I was working as a porter at a hotel; the wages were not good, and I was desperate to escape the life of poverty and drudgery that had been my father's miserable existence.'

Vadim's face hardened. 'I would have done anything—and, trust me, there was a thriving black market operated by criminal gangs who lured young, dissatisfied men into their fold with the promise of easy money. But I was lucky.' He shrugged. 'At the hotel I met a German businessman who owned a chain of toy shops across Europe. One day he asked me about the traditional Russian dolls he had seen, and voiced an interest in stocking them in his shops. By that evening I had sourced a supply of dolls and negotiated a deal with Herr Albrecht to act as his supplier. That was the beginning of my career. Within a couple of years I had made enough money to be able to invest in other ventures. The gap in the mobile phone industry was waiting to be filled, and I seized the opportunity.'

'You make it sound easy,' Ella murmured, utterly transfixed by the story of Vadim's route to success. 'But I'm sure it can't have been. You must have made personal sacrifices.' She hesitated, and then said quietly, 'I sometimes feel that when I was growing up I sacrificed many of the things that other young people take for granted. Music demanded so much of my time that I rarely socialised with kids of my own age, and now my career is so consuming that I have virtually no time for friends or…' she hesitated fractionally '…relationships.' She gave him a faint smile. 'I wonder if one day we'll look back and wonder if the dreams we chased so hard were worth the heartache?'

There was a depth to Ella that he had never found in any other woman, Vadim mused darkly. Her insight was uncomfortably close to the mark, but she had no idea that he had sacrificed the happiness and ultimately the lives of his wife and child on the altar of his ambition.

Had the single-minded determination he'd given to chasing his dreams been worth it? He now had wealth beyond anything he had ever imagined when he'd made that first deal with Herr Albrecht all those years ago. But sometimes, in the dark hour before dawn, when he surfaced from the regular nightmare that had haunted him for the past ten years and heard the echo of Klara's terrified screams for him to save her, he knew he would gladly give up everything he owned to hold his daughter in his arms once again.

Tak-Sin had prepared an exotic fruit salad for dessert, and Ella helped herself to slices of mango and passion fruit, relishing the sweet, fresh flavours on her tongue. Vadim shook his head when she offered him the fruit bowl, and instead drained his champagne glass and refilled it. He had lapsed into silence—a brooding silence she felt reluctant to break. She sensed that his thoughts were far away, and she wondered what memories from his past had caused him to look so grim.

The weather seemed to be reflecting his mood. While they had been eating the evening sunshine had been replaced by ominous-looking clouds, and now the air was still and heavy, the atmosphere charged with electricity that made the tiny hairs on Ella's arms stand on end. Through the French doors she saw the sky was black, and she caught her breath when lightning seared the heavens and briefly filled the room with brilliant white light. She flinched when a low growl of thunder sounded from across the river.

'I hate storms,' she admitted shakily as Vadim returned from wherever his thoughts had taken him and focused his piercing blue gaze on her. 'When I was a child, one of the gardeners at Stafford Hall was struck and killed by lightning.'

He frowned. 'You saw it happen?'

'Oh, no—fortunately; but it was all the other staff talked about for weeks afterwards. They said his violent death would mean another ghost would haunt the Hall.'

'Did you have many staff?' Vadim asked curiously. 'I've seen photographs of Stafford Hall and it looks a vast place.'

Ella nodded, thinking of the great grey-walled house with the stone gargoyles over the front door that had given her nightmares as a little girl. 'It is—seventeen bedrooms, numerous reception rooms and a chapel in the grounds where it was rumoured that a priest was murdered on the orders of the King, hundreds of years ago. When my father first inherited the Hall from my grandfather we had a small army of cooks, butlers and maids, but as the money ran out he sacked the staff until there was only the housekeeper, Mrs Rogers, left. She was about a hundred,' Ella added ruefully, 'but she helped to care for my mother, and as my father wanted as little to do with Mama as possible, he allowed dear Betty to stay.'

Thunder rumbled again, louder this time, so that it seemed to reverberate around the room. 'Did you believe the house was haunted?' Vadim murmured, sensing Ella's tension as the storm approached.

She hesitated, and then gave a reluctant nod. 'I was a very imaginative child, and because my mother was often unwell I spent a lot of time on my own. I convinced myself that the stories I'd heard about the headless baron and the Grey Lady, who was said to have been stabbed to death by her cruel husband, were true. The room at the top of the tower where she was supposed to have met her death was thought to be the most haunted room in the house. It was always cold, and none of the staff would go up there.' She paused again, and then revealed in a low tone, 'My father used to lock me in that room as punishment for any misdemeanour I committed. And, as I only had to walk into the same room as him to incur his annoyance, I was punished pretty often when he was home.'

Vadim felt a violent surge of dislike for Ella's father. 'Did he know you were scared?'

'Oh, yes,' Ella said grimly. 'I would be hysterical with fear when he dragged me up there—that's why he enjoyed doing it. Refined cruelty was his forte.'

It was obvious that Ella had feared her father as much as she had feared the ghosts she had believed roamed her childhood home, and some indefinable emotion tugged on Vadim's heart as he imagined her as a terrified little girl. 'Did he ever punish you physically?' he asked harshly.

Ella gave a start as a thunderclap shook the room, and she glanced nervously out at the black starless sky that seemed to smother the garden beneath a heavy cloak. 'No,' she said slowly. 'He never hit me, but sometimes my mother would have bruises… She always said she'd fallen, or banged into the door… But I knew it had been *him*. Fortunately he never stayed at the Hall for long. He only came back from his house in France when he was short of money and needed to sell off another family heirloom, and it was a huge relief when he went away again.'

'But if your father treated your mother so badly, why did she remain married to him?'

It was a question Ella has asked herself countless times,

and she had never come to terms with the only answer she'd ever been able to come up with. 'I suppose she loved him,' she said at last. 'She once told me that she had fallen in love with him the moment they met, and I think that whatever he did, however many times he broke her heart with his infidelity and his indifference, she never stopped loving him.' She shook her head. 'My mother was such a sweet, gentle person. I don't understand why my father didn't love her the way she loved him,' she cried angrily.

'Maybe he couldn't,' Vadim said quietly. He stared unseeingly across the dark garden while the familiar demon, guilt, stirred from its slumber. Irina had been gentle, and her sweet, shy smile had been the first thing he had noticed about her each time he'd walked into the grocery store where she had worked. He *had* loved her, he assured himself, but the painful truth was that he hadn't loved her enough. He had known he was the centre of her world, but, much as it shamed him to admit it, she hadn't been his.

His business, the pursuit of wealth and success, had been his mistress. He had not been unfaithful to his wife, as Ella's father had been to her mother, but could he really say he had been a better husband than Earl Stafford when he had not spent enough time with Irina and Klara?

'The reason he didn't love her was because he was selfish and only cared about his own interests,' Ella said bitterly.

Her words echoed in Vadim's head and his guilt choked him.

Ella shivered. 'I never want to be like my mother and fall in love with someone so desperately that I lose my pride and self-worth. Loving my father didn't make Mama happy, and ultimately I believe it destroyed her. No man is worth that,' she stated fiercely.

As she spoke, lightning zig-zagged across the sky and the crash of accompanying thunder was so loud that she screamed and dropped the glass of water she had just picked up. It smashed on impact with the tiled floor, but as she jumped out of her chair and bent to collect the shards Vadim strode around the table and pulled her to her feet. The room was plunged into darkness as the wall-lamps went out; the candles continued to flicker bravely for a few seconds before a gust of wind whipped through the open doors and snuffed out the flames.

'It must be a power cut. Wait there while I find a torch.'

He was back within seconds, shining the torchlight in front of him as he took Ella's hand and guided her over the broken glass. 'I'll clear it up later, when the power's restored.'

The storm was directly overhead now, and thunder boomed like pagan drums while the darkness was rent apart periodically by flashes of lightning. Vadim could feel the tremors running through Ella as he led her over to the French doors and turned her so that she was looking out over the garden. 'The power of the elements is awesome, but you are safe from the storm here with me,' he murmured, sliding his arms around her waist and drawing her close, so that her back was pressed up against his chest.

From the storm outside, perhaps, Ella thought shakily. But her instincts screamed that she was not safe from Vadim—or herself. The storm raging inside her was equally violent as the tumult in the skies above, and the pressure of Vadim's hard thighs pushing against her bottom evoked a burning heat in her pelvis. She could feel the erratic beat of his heart, and it seemed to pulse through her own veins as the drumbeat of desire thudding through her built to a crescendo.

He was a man like her father, warned a voice in her head, a heartless playboy who used women and discarded them when he had tired of them. But she could no longer deny the sexual chemistry that had simmered between them since the night they had met in Paris and was now at combustion point.

There was no danger she would fall in love with him, she assured herself, desire shivering through her when he pushed her hair aside and trailed his lips up her neck to the sensitive spot beneath her ear. She would never repeat the mistake her mother had made. The hard ridge of his arousal nudging insistently between the cleft of her buttocks was irrefutable proof of his hunger for her, and at this moment, as the storm crashed and trembled around them, her whole being quivered with the need for him to assuage the longing inside her that was as old and insistent as mankind.

CHAPTER SEVEN

HE NEEDED a woman tonight. Correction—he needed *this* woman, Vadim acknowledged as he turned Ella to face him and stared at the tremulous softness of her lips. He did not want to dwell on the past, and he had learned that the future was never assured. For him, the here and now was all that mattered, and at this moment the urge to make love to Ella burned like a fever in his blood. He slid his hand beneath her hair, the feel of the soft silky strands against his skin causing a sharp stab of desire in his gut, and with a muttered oath he cupped her nape and brought his mouth down on hers.

A lightning flare lit up the room and threw the sharp angles and planes of Vadim's face into stark relief. He seemed so remote and forbidding that for a second Ella felt a surge of fear, but the first brush of his mouth and the bold thrust of his tongue between her lips obliterated any lingering doubts that this was where she wanted to be. Desire licked through her veins like wildfire, heating her blood and making every nerve-ending so exquisitely sensitive that she moaned when he cupped her breast in his palm and stroked his thumbpad over the taut nipple straining beneath her silk dress.

He deepened the kiss, taking it to another level that was flagrantly erotic, and she melted against him and wound her

The Reader Service—Here's how it works: Accepting your 2 free books and 2 free gifts (gifts valued at approximately $10.00) places you under no obligation to buy anything. You may keep the books and gifts and return the shipping statement marked "cancel". If you do not cancel, about a month later we'll send you 6 additional books and bill you just $4.05 each for the regular-print edition or $4.55 each for the larger-print edition in the U.S. or $4.74 each for the regular-print edition or $5.24 each for the larger-print edition in Canada. That is a savings of at least 13% off the cover price. It's quite a bargain! Shipping and handling is just 50¢ per book in the U.S. and 75¢ per book in Canada.* You may cancel at any time, but if you choose to continue, every month we'll send you 6 more books, which you may either purchase at the discount price or return to us and cancel your subscription.
*Terms and prices subject to change without notice. Prices do not include applicable taxes. Sales tax applicable in N.Y. Canadian residents will be charged applicable provincial taxes and GST. Offer not valid in Quebec. Credit or debit balances in a customer's account(s) may be offset by any other outstanding balance owed by or to the customer. Please allow 4 to 6 weeks for delivery. Offer available while quantities last. All orders subject to approval.

▶ If offer card is missing write to: The Reader Service, P.O. Box 1867, Buffalo, NY 14240-1867 or visit www.ReaderService.com ▶

NO POSTAGE
NECESSARY
IF MAILED
IN THE
UNITED STATES

BUSINESS REPLY MAIL
FIRST-CLASS MAIL   PERMIT NO. 717   BUFFALO, NY

POSTAGE WILL BE PAID BY ADDRESSEE

THE READER SERVICE
PO BOX 1867
BUFFALO NY 14240-9952

Send For
2 FREE BOOKS
Today!

I accept your offer!

Please send me two free *Harlequin Presents®* novels and two mystery gifts (gifts worth about $10). I understand that these books are completely free—even the shipping and handling will be paid—and I am under no obligation to purchase anything, ever, as explained on the back of this card.

About how many NEW paperback fiction books have you purchased in the past 3 months?

❏ 0-2
E4EM

❏ 3-6
E4EX

❏ 7 or more
E4FA

❏ I prefer the regular-print edition
106/306 HDL

❏ I prefer the larger-print edition
176/376 HDL

Please Print

FIRST NAME

LAST NAME

ADDRESS

APT.#   CITY

STATE/PROV.   ZIP/POSTAL CODE

Visit us online at
www.ReaderService.com

arms around his neck, her eyes flying open when she felt the floor suddenly disappear from beneath her feet.

'Guide me,' he commanded roughly as he scooped her into his arms, collected the torch from the table and handed it to her.

'Where are we going?' she asked shakily.

'Bed.'

His desire for Ella had spiralled out of control, Vadim acknowledged grimly. Last night he had listened to the voice of his conscience, but tonight he could not resist her. Perhaps it was the pagan power of the storm, or perhaps it was her revelations about how her father had terrified her as a child that had induced this primal feeling to protect her and claim her as his woman. All he knew was that tonight he was driven by an instinct as old as mankind to make love to her.

The hungry gleam in Vadim's eyes caused Ella's heart to skitter in her chest. 'If you object, now is the time to say so,' he warned her as he strode out of the room and across the hall to the stairs.

Her brain told her she should demand that he set her on her feet, bid him goodnight and return to her part of the house— but her body ached with a need that decimated her thought processes and robbed her of words. Talking about her childhood had reminded her of how much she had hated her father, but she was no longer a child, and she was shocked to realise how much she had allowed her feelings about Earl Stafford to affect her adult life. He was the reason she was terrified of falling in love, the reason she had always frozen off any man who had shown an interest in her, and why she was still a virgin. But she was damned if she would allow her hatred of her father to dictate her actions any more, she thought fiercely. She was an independent woman who was capable of making her own choices, and tonight she chose to have her first sexual experience with Vadim.

But despite her brave avowal her heart thudded unevenly as he climbed the stairs. The torchlight flickered over the pale walls of the upper landing and the artwork she had chosen. She knew every inch of Kingfisher House and had decorated every room—including the master bedroom, with its huge bed covered in a navy satin bedspread that matched the colour of the carpet and complemented the ivory silk wallpaper.

The doors leading to the balcony were open, the sounds of the storm outside clearly audible, but Ella was conscious of nothing but Vadim when he lowered her onto the bed and immediately stretched out next to her. The only source of light in the room was the glow from the torch, casting shadows on the ceiling, but he found her mouth with unerring precision and covered it with his own, moving his lips on hers with feverish need and demanding a response she was powerless to deny.

Above the angry growls of thunder she could hear the ragged sound of her breathing. Her heart was pounding as her whole body was gripped with a need she could barely comprehend. The ache deep in her pelvis had become a relentless throbbing that caused her to arch her hips in a desperate invitation for Vadim to touch her and caress her…

When he finally broke the kiss and lifted his head to stare down at her she traced her tongue over her swollen lips. One kiss was not enough, she wanted more, and she slid her fingers into his thick black hair to urge him down on her. But instead of claiming her mouth he trailed his lips down her throat, to the pulse beating frenetically at its base.

'Your skin feels like satin,' he growled, his voice rough with desire. He began to unfasten the buttons that ran down the front of her dress, and Ella caught her breath when he pushed the silvery-grey silk aside to expose her high, firm breasts. 'Beautiful,' he muttered rawly. He cupped the twin mounds in his palms and revelled in their softness before he lowered his head and flicked his tongue across one nipple, so that it instantly swelled and hardened. The sensation was so exquisite that Ella could not restrain her startled cry of pleasure. No man had ever touched her as Vadim was doing, and when he transferred his attention to her other breast and drew the sensitive peak fully into his mouth she trembled with reaction.

He gave a ragged laugh when she gripped his hair and held his head against her breast, desperate for him to continue the erotic caress. 'Do you like that? I knew that beneath the ice-maiden act I'd find a sensual sex kitten,' he murmured, unable to disguise his satisfaction. Her open enjoyment of his mouth on her breasts was a massive turn-on, but it put paid to his plan for a leisurely seduction, Vadim acknowledged self-derisively. His arousal was rock-hard, and throbbing with impatience for him to spread her beneath him and plunge between her pale thighs. He had wanted her from the moment he'd laid eyes on her, but she had made him wait. It wasn't surprising that his body was taut with desire—a desire that grew more urgent when he dragged her dress over her hips to reveal her pale, slender body; naked but for the pair of grey lace knickers that hid her femininity from his gaze.

He felt the tremor that ran through her when he traced his lips down over her flat stomach and dipped his tongue into the delicate recess of her navel. He wanted to take his time exploring each delightful dip and curve, but his feverish need was clamouring to be assuaged and he continued lower, hooking his fingers in the waistband of her knickers and tugging them down her legs with one deft movement.

Ella felt a moment's panic when Vadim stared down at her body. It was the first time any man had seen her naked, and while the heat in his brilliant blue gaze was flattering, his undisguised hunger sent a frisson of apprehension through her. She was about to give her virginity to this enigmatic, brooding man who was almost a stranger to her. Suddenly she was beset by doubts, and tensed when he slipped his hand between her legs.

Ella's neat triangle of pale blonde curls was silky soft against Vadim's fingers, and the delicate scent of her arousal inflamed his senses so that he barely registered that she had stiffened. Driven by a primitive, powerful urge, he eased her thighs apart and ran his finger lightly up and down the lips of her vagina until they swelled and slowly opened, like the petals of a flower unfolding, to reveal her moist, damp heat.

Ella gasped when she felt Vadim probe the slick wetness between her legs and her fear faded. Lost in the world of sensory pleasure he had evoked, she was beyond conscious thought, her whole being focused intently on each new sensation that he created with his wickedly inventive hands. The feather-light brush of his thumbpad across her ultra-sensitive clitoris made her cry out, her breath coming in sharp little gasps when he gently parted her and slid his finger deep into her welcoming heat.

'Please…' She did not know what she was pleading for, only that his erotic exploration with one finger, and then two, easing into her and caressing her with skilful precision, was creating a raging tumult inside her that was rapidly spiralling out of control.

Abruptly Vadim ended the mind-blowing foreplay and muttered something in Russian as he sprang up from the bed. 'I can't wait either,' he admitted harshly. She had tormented his dreams for too many nights, and the sight of her pale beauty, her hair falling in silky disarray over her shoulders, brushing against her small breasts with their swollen, dusky nipples, drove everything from his mind but his desperation to take her hard and fast and reach the sexual nirvana that he knew instinctively he would find with her.

He shrugged out of his clothes with urgent movements

that lacked his usual grace, his gaze locked with Ella's as he stripped. His shirt fell carelessly to the floor, swiftly followed by his trousers. Satisfaction and a heightened sense of anticipation surged through him when he stepped out of his boxers and heard her sharply indrawn breath as she stared with flattering fascination at the jutting length of his arousal.

The only naked male body Ella had ever seen had been sculpted from marble and standing in an art gallery. Vadim's body was more beautiful than any sculpture, she thought, her mouth suddenly dry as her eyes moved over his broad chest, gleaming like polished bronze in the torchlight and overlaid with a covering of wiry black hair that arrowed down over his flat stomach. Heart pounding, she dropped her gaze lower still and felt a jolt of shock when she absorbed the awesome strength of his erection. He was all hard, muscular male, and as he walked purposefully back to the bed she tensed. What was she *doing*? the voice of doubt in her head demanded. She knew of Vadim's reputation as a playboy—she must have been mad to have allowed things to get this far.

'Are you going to live like a nun for the rest of your life?' Jenny's words taunted her. No, she denied fiercely, she did not want to remain a virgin for ever. Nor was she saving her virginity for when she fell in love. Love was an illusion. But the instant she had seen Vadim across a crowded room in Paris she had fallen in lust, and at twenty-four it was high time she discarded her innocence.

Vadim knelt on the bed, leaned over Ella and captured her lips in a hard, hungry kiss, sliding his tongue into her mouth in an erotic mimicry of how he would soon drive his throbbing shaft into the welcoming slick heat of her femininity. Next time he would take the leisurely route and taste her honeyed sweetness with his mouth, maybe tease the tight nub of her clitoris with his tongue until he brought her to the edge of ecstasy. He would encourage her to touch him too. But right now just the thought of her slender fingers encircling him intensified his arousal, so that he feared he was about to explode with the hot, pulsing need that made his entire body shake.

He broke the kiss briefly to reach into the bedside drawer, and donned protection with swift efficiency before he positioned himself over her and nudged her thighs apart. The faint wariness in her eyes made him pause for a second, but his blood was pounding through his veins, his desire for her an unstoppable force, urging him to surge forward. He slid his hands beneath her bottom, lifted her hips and entered her with one powerful thrust—and instantly stilled when he felt the tear of a fragile membrane and heard her shocked cry of pain.

For a few seconds he stared at her in stunned incomprehension which swiftly turned to anger as his brain accepted the indisputable truth. 'Your first time?' he demanded harshly. He swore savagely in Russian. 'What the devil are you playing at, Ella?'

'I'm not playing at anything,' she denied falteringly, shaken by his reaction. Perhaps naïvely, she had not expected her initiation into sex to be quite so uncomfortable. When Vadim had penetrated her untutored body she had felt a sharp, stinging pain, but already it was fading, and the restless ache in her pelvis was once more clamouring to be assuaged. She could not hide her confusion when he abruptly withdrew from her, and she tentatively placed her hand on his arm, thinking that he was angry with himself for hurting her. 'Vadim, it's all right...'

'The hell it is,' he bit out savagely. His facial muscles were so taut that he looked as though he had been carved from granite, and Ella's stomach dipped as she realised that he wasn't angry with himself, but with her. 'If I'd had any idea you were a virgin I would never have taken you to bed.'

He closed his eyes and in his mind he saw Irina. He had been her first lover, and making love to her on their wedding night had been a special experience for both of them. With Ella it was simply sex. But he was aware that her first time should have been special, with someone who cared for her, and he felt guilty that he had unwittingly stolen her virginity. She had chosen to sleep with him, he reminded himself. But he hoped she did not think his emotions were involved, because she meant nothing to him.

The heated passion in Ella's veins quickly cooled, leaving her feeling shivery, and sick with mortification. There was no hint of the hungry desire that had blazed in Vadim's eyes when he had carried her up to his bedroom, and she felt stupid and embarrassed that she hadn't warned him of her inexperience.

He rolled away from her and swung his legs over the side of the bed, raking his hand through his dark hair as he struggled to control his simmering frustration. From the moment they had first met the chemistry between them had been explosive, and her passionate response to his kisses had given no indication that she had never had a lover. He turned his head to stare at her slender body, her skin milky-pale against the blue silk bedspread and her small, pert breasts pouting at him, tempting him to close his mouth around her nipples and feel them harden against his tongue. Desire clawed in his gut but he forced himself to ignore it.

'Why did you do it?' he asked coldly.

Ella bit her lip. 'I…I didn't think it would matter. The fact that it's my first time means nothing to me.' She quickly looked away from him, stunned by the realisation that she had lied and that she had wanted him to be her first lover. She barely knew him, she thought despairingly, and this feeling that he was the other half of her soul was utterly ridiculous.

'Really?' He gave a sardonic laugh. 'Are you sure you did

not think that I would somehow be honoured that you had given your virginity to me? Because if you did, I'm afraid I must disappoint you. I don't want a sacrificial lamb in my bed,' he continued harshly, ignoring her swiftly indrawn breath. 'I only bed experienced, sexually confident women, and I have neither the time nor the patience to tutor a naïve girl—especially when there is the added danger that you might fall in love with me.'

'My God—you arrogant *jerk*!' Trembling with humiliated rage, Ella sat bolt-upright, the violent movement causing her breasts to bounce provocatively, so that she quickly dragged the silk coverlet over them, her cheeks burning. 'I would never fall in love with you—' She broke off, blinking dazedly when his face was suddenly illuminated. For a second she could not understand what had happened, but then she realised that the power had been restored and the timer on the bedside lamps had been activated. The room seemed painfully bright after the dark, and the furious expression on Vadim's face made her want to weep with shame.

From outside came the sound of rain—big, heavy drops, falling slowly at first as the stormclouds broke. A gust of wind whipped in from the balcony and tugged at the curtains, and with a muttered oath Vadim got up and strode across the room to close the doors. Ella stared at the masculine beauty of his naked body, trailing her eyes over his wide shoulders and then down to his waist, hips, and finally his buttocks and long, muscular legs. Minutes ago he had lowered himself onto her and pushed her legs apart with one hair-roughened thigh, and the stark memory fanned the flames of the hot, pulsing need inside her that refused to die.

What was she going to do—beg him to take her? she asked herself raggedly. Her self-respect was in shreds, and the realisation that her body still ached for his possession, even after his scathing comments that he did not want to bed a virgin, filled her with panic. His rejection hurt, she acknowledged miserably. But she would rather die than let him see it. She had to get away from him. He had closed the doors to the balcony and was drawing the curtains across them. Any second now he would turn around... Frantically she snatched up her dress and dragged it over her head. There was no time to gather her shoes or knickers; she simply fled out of the door and down the stairs, not pausing when she heard him call her name.

The door to her part of the house was locked. She rattled the handle in frustration, remembering how she had bolted it earlier in the day, when she had discovered that Vadim was the new tenant of Kingfisher House. She heard his footsteps on the landing above and raced through the dining room and out onto the terrace. The rain was falling so hard that it stung her skin, but instead of running along the terrace to the French doors leading to her flat, she turned and sped across the lawn, desperate to put as much space between her and her tormentor as possible.

The lights from the house spilled halfway down the garden, but the decked patio beside the river was in darkness, broken only occasionally when the scudding clouds parted to allow the moon to glimmer across the water. Ella stared down at the swirling river while the rain lashed her and mingled with the angry tears streaming down her face. First thing tomorrow she would phone Jenny and ask if she could stay with her until she found somewhere to live—because she would rather die than have to face Vadim ever again.

'What are you doing out here? The rain's like a goddamned monsoon.'

His angry voice sounded behind her, and she spun round, lost her balance and almost fell into the fast-flowing river.

Uttering a curse that singed her ears, Vadim sprang forward

and snatched her into his arms. 'Watch your step. You could be swept away, you little fool.'

Fury replaced the fear that had surged through him when he had seen her standing so close to the water's edge. For a second he had thought she would fall, and he knew he would have had little chance of dragging her from the swirling current before she was swept away. He could not stand another death on his conscience.

When he had first realised that Ella had run from the bedroom he'd had no intention of following her. She hadn't been honest with him, and he'd felt angry that he had been tricked into a situation he would never have chosen. He did not want the responsibility of being her first lover. But he had been tormented by the expression on her face when he had rejected her. The flash of hurt in her eyes had been uncannily similar to the look on Irina's face during one of their many arguments about how he spent too much time at work rather than with her.

Ella should have told him she was a virgin, but the knowledge that he had been unnecessarily cruel had seen him drag on his trousers and chase after her. Now, as he stared down at her rain-drenched form and felt the violent shivers that ripped through her, an indefinable feeling tugged in his chest.

Vadim's scathing tone was the last straw, and the fact that he still looked gorgeous, even when his hair was plastered to his head, the rain running in streams down his bare chest and moulding his trousers to his thighs, set fire to Ella's temper.

'I must be a fool to have had anything to do with you,' she yelled as she fought free of his hold. The memory of how he had rejected her burned like acid in her gut, and in an agony of embarrassment she lashed out at him, beating her hands against his chest until he caught both her wrists in his vice-like grip.

'Be still, you little wildcat,' he ordered harshly, snaking his other arm around her waist to haul her away from the river's edge. He was breathing hard, his nostrils flaring as he fought the urge to claim her mouth and kiss her into submission. Ella shook her head, so that her wet hair whipped across his face, and she gave a cry of frustration when she failed to free her wrists from his grasp. The driving rain had soaked through her dress so that the grey silk moulded her body like a second skin, and as she squirmed furiously against him the feel of her pebble-hard nipples dragging against his chest drove Vadim to the edge of sexual insanity.

'*Let go of me.*' Ella had to shout above the sound of the rain beating against the wooden decking, but she had spent so much of her life keeping quiet, keeping her mouth shut so as not to annoy her father, that shouting was a revelation which restored a little of her pride. She was no longer a scared little shadow, flitting about Stafford Hall, she thought as she lifted her head and glared at Vadim. She was a grown woman, and she was hurt and humiliated and as angry as hell. 'Just so you know—there's not the slightest chance I would *ever* fall in love with you,' she flung at him. 'I didn't choose you to be my first lover because I harboured some stupid idea that emotions would be involved. I *know* what kind of a man you are. You're a notorious playboy, and I would never make the mistake that your last girlfriend, Kelly Adams, made, by hoping to touch your heart, because I'm well aware that you don't have one.'

'Is that so?' he gritted, hauling her so hard against him that their bodies were welded together while the rain continued to hammer down on them. He'd had a heart once, he recalled bitterly, anger surging through him at Ella's accusation that he was an immoral womaniser, intent only on seeking his own pleasure. She had no idea that his heart had been torn apart. The pain of losing his wife and daughter had been unbearable, and he had vowed never to lay himself open to such agony ever again.

'The only reason I decided to sleep with you was because you push all the right buttons,' Ella continued wildly. 'You were right when you said the sexual chemistry between us blazed from the moment we met, and all I ever wanted from you tonight was your sexual expertise.'

She knew a moment's triumph when Vadim released her wrists, but seconds later she gasped when he lifted her off the ground and held her so tightly against him that she could feel the rock-solid length of his arousal pushing against her pelvis.

'Well, if that's really all you want, who am I to deny you, angel face?' he drawled mockingly.

'Put me down. I mean it, Vadim.' Panic sharpened her voice when he ignored her plea and strode across the decking towards the summerhouse. 'I'm tired of playing games.' Once again she tried to fight her way out of his arms, but he was too strong for her. He carried her as easily as if she were a rag-doll, and as the warmth of his body seeped into her, and his heart slammed in time with her own, the fight drained out of her. Desire flowed like molten lava through her veins as she clung to his shoulders and wrapped her legs around his thighs, so that with each step he took the jutting hardness of his erection strained against his trousers and nudged insistently between her legs.

'You're right; the time for games is over,' he growled as he shouldered the door of the summerhouse, stepped inside and immediately bent his head to capture her mouth in a devastatingly sensual kiss that drove the breath from Ella's body.

It was a statement of possession and a warning of intent, his tongue thrusting between her lips with such erotic skill that resistance was impossible. But her pride demanded that she should try. 'I thought you said you don't bed virgins?' she reminded him savagely, when he finally lifted his lips from hers.

'I'm prepared to make an exception for you.' His wicked smile revealed his white teeth and reminded her of a wolf about to devour its prey. The summerhouse was dark, but his eyes gleamed with a fierce determination as he dragged the cushions from the garden chairs, spread them on the floor and lowered her onto them.

She should push him away, Ella thought desperately. But her hands seemed to be drawn of their own volition to the muscular strength of his chest, and she brushed her fingertips through the dark whorls of hair that covered his satiny skin. Earlier he had aroused her body to the very edge of fulfilment, and the abrupt halt to their lovemaking had left her aching with a need that only he could appease.

The combination of slippery wet silk and tiny buttons running down the front of her dress tested Vadim's patience to its limits—until with a muttered oath he gripped the fragile material and ripped it to the waist, exposing her naked breasts to his hungry gaze. She was shivering with cold and intense excitement, and the first hard strokes of his tongue lashing one nipple and then the other made her cry out and arch her back, so that he drew one tight nub fully into his mouth and sucked until the pleasure was almost unendurable.

The fire inside her was burning out of control, his earlier rejection and the scalding humiliation she had felt when she had fled from him forgotten in the maelstrom of sensations he was inciting with his hands and mouth. Her heart slammed beneath her ribs when he dragged the hem of her dress up so that it bunched around her waist, but she made no attempt to stop him when he pushed her legs apart and slid his finger into her slick wetness. Her heightened state of arousal from his earlier caresses had not faded and she was instantly ready for him. But, although he was more turned on than he had ever been in his life, Vadim was determined not to rush her. She had taunted him that the reason she had chosen him as her first lover was for his sexual expertise, and he was not going to disappoint her.

Ella gave a moan of protest when Vadim lifted his mouth from her breast, and then gasped when he moved down her body and she felt his warm breath against her thigh.

'No…' Utterly shocked by the first brush of his tongue against her swollen vaginal lips, she instinctively tried to bring her legs together, but he held them firmly apart and continued the intimate caress with a ruthless efficiency that brought her to the very edge of sexual ecstasy.

By the time he lifted his head she was mindless with desire, and when his hand moved to his waist she sat up and helped him drag his wet trousers over his hips. The throbbing length of his erection filled her hands and she stroked him tentatively—until he groaned and pushed her onto her back.

'It has to be now, angel,' he muttered, drawing on all his formidable willpower to slow the pace and rub his swollen shaft gently against her, until she opened and he entered her with one slow, careful thrust.

There was no pain this time. Just an incredible feeling of fullness as Vadim slid deeper and then withdrew almost completely. For a split second Ella was terrified that he was going to leave her again, and she dug her fingers into his shoulders to anchor her to him. His rough laugh told her he understood her fear, and he surged forward and drew back, sliding deeper with each thrust as he taught her the age-old rhythm that took her higher and higher, until she felt as though she were teetering on the edge of some dark and mysterious place, trembling with desperation to discover its secrets.

He slid his hand beneath her bottom and tilted her hips, and each powerful thrust suddenly became even more intense. 'Vadim!' She cried his name and clung to him, almost afraid of the cataclysmic explosion of pleasure that ripped through her as she experienced her first orgasm. It was awesome and utterly indescribable. Nothing had prepared her for the exquisite spasms that radiated out from her central core and enveloped her entire body in a feeling of complete ecstasy. And as she arched beneath him and sobbed his name she heard the low groan that seemed to be torn from his throat and felt him tense, poised above her, his blue eyes locked with hers for timeless seconds, before he gave one final, savage thrust and threw his head back, his face a taut mask and his big body shuddering with the force of his climax.

The sound of the rain beating down on the summerhouse slowly impinged on Vadim's brain and dragged him reluctantly from his deeply relaxed state. It felt good lying here, cocooned in the soft darkness and shielded from the wild elements outside. His body was still joined with Ella's—and that felt more than good, he acknowledged ruefully. It felt amazing. The tight sheath of her vaginal muscles held him in a velvet embrace, and already he could feel himself hardening again. But he should not have made love to her without protection even once, and it would be criminally irresponsible to compound the mistake.

Ignoring the tug of regret in his gut, he withdrew from her and rolled onto his side. The rain was easing, and in the silver moonlight glimmering through the window she looked pale and ethereal, with her wet hair streaming around her shoulders. But the stunned expression in her eyes made him grimace. He had not planned to make love to her. The discovery of her innocence had put her off-limits as far as he was concerned, and his sole intention when he had chased after her was to ensure her safety. But from the second he had pulled her into his arms, away from the edge of the swirling river, and held her trembling body against him, he had been lost.

No woman had ever got to him the way Ella did, nor aroused him to the point that his usual cool logic was replaced with mindless, fevered desire. Even the knowledge that she was a virgin had no longer mattered, he thought grimly. Driven by his desperate hunger for her, he had followed the dictates of his body rather than his brain as passion had overwhelmed him. But now guilt tore at him.

'Did I hurt you?' he asked roughly.

Ella's eyes flew to Vadim's face. 'No,' she said truthfully. There had been no pain this time, just a wondrous feeling of fullness as he had joined his body with hers. 'You ruined my dress, though,' she added, blushing as she dragged the grey silk across her breasts and discovered that every button was missing.

His slow smile stole her breath. 'I'll buy you a new one.' He stood up, held out his hand to help her to her feet, and then to her shock scooped her up into his arms.

'I can walk,' Ella protested as he stepped out of the sum-merhouse and strode up to the house, apparently unconcerned that he was stark naked. It was lucky that Kingfisher House was not overlooked by neighbours, she thought as she clung to his shoulders. Her heart lurched when he walked straight past the doors leading to her flat, on into the main house, where he climbed the stairs and carried her through the master bedroom to the *en suite* bathroom.

'I should go back to my room,' she murmured when he set her on her feet and slid her torn dress over her shoulders. The walk back to the house through the rain had cooled her skin, and shock at her wanton behaviour in the summerhouse was setting in, so that she felt a ridiculous urge to cry. In those moments when Vadim had taken her to the very pinnacle of pleasure she had felt as though their hearts had become one. But of course it was an illusion—because if Vadim had a heart he kept it under lock and key, and she would never be so foolish as to fall for a playboy who viewed women as a means of entertainment. 'I'm all in,' she whispered as her dress slithered to the floor and his brilliant blue eyes blazed over her naked body.

'I know,' he said, and the unexpected gentleness in his voice tugged at Ella's heart. Her eyes were huge in her delicate face, and she looked achingly vulnerable. He should have taken her to her room and bade her goodnight. But for reasons he refused to decipher he'd wanted her with him. She was shivering with cold, and he lifted her and carried her into the shower. 'This will warm you up, and then you can sleep,' he promised, smiling at her shocked expression when he picked up the bar of soap and began to smooth it over her breasts.

By the time Vadim had soaped every inch of her body, shampooed her hair and held her against him while the spray rinsed them both, Ella was tingling all over, and his ministrations with a towel caused molten heat to surge through her veins. The feeling of being cared for was dangerously beguiling, she acknowledged when he carried her through to the bedroom, slid into bed beside her and drew the sheet around them. They'd had fantastic sex, but it meant nothing to either of them, she reminded herself firmly. But when he drew her into his arms, so that her head was resting on his chest, a feeling of utter contentment stole over her and she fell asleep, unaware that he remained awake watching her for long into the night.

CHAPTER EIGHT

ELLA was awoken by the gentle breeze which stirred the voile curtains. The doors were ajar, revealing a cloudless blue sky, but her eyes were drawn to Vadim, who was standing on the balcony, staring out over the garden. He was dressed in a superbly tailored suit and looked devastatingly handsome, but his stern profile made him seem so remote and forbidding that it was almost impossible to believe he was the same man who had woken her just before dawn and made passionate love to her.

Just thinking about how skilfully he had aroused her with his hands and mouth made her blush, and as he turned and stepped into the bedroom she was acutely conscious that she was naked beneath the silk sheet.

'What time is it?' she murmured, wishing she knew the protocol for greeting the man you'd spent the night having great sex with, but who seemed to have turned into a stranger in the cold light of day.

He flicked back the sleeve of his jacket and glanced at his watch. 'Just after eight.'

Ella gave a yelp as reality hit with a vengeance. 'I have to be at rehearsals at nine. Gustav blows a fuse if any of the orchestra members are late.' She jerked upright, the rosy colour in her cheeks deepening as she dislodged the sheet and Vadim's eyes immediately dropped to her bare breasts.

'Where are the rehearsals?'

'Cadogan Hall, near Sloane Square,' she mumbled as she snatched the sheet around her.

Vadim strolled over to the wall of wardrobes, opened a door and selected a robe from several that were hanging inside. 'Here,' he said, walking back to the bed and handing it to her. 'It'll probably swamp you. I'm afraid I don't have anything in your petite size.'

'Thank you.' Ella took the robe and glanced across at the others in the wardrobe, startled by the realisation that he kept bathrobes in a variety of sizes—presumably for the occasions when he invited a woman to spend the night with him. It was extremely thoughtful of him, she reminded herself, trying to ignore the heavy feeling in the pit of her stomach that she was just another blonde who was passing through his bedroom.

'My offices are not far from Cadogan Hall, so I can give you a lift. What time will you finish tonight?'

'The orchestra will finish late afternoon, but I have additional rehearsals for my solo performance coming up in Paris, and I don't suppose I'll get away until at least six o'clock.'

Vadim shrugged. 'Fine. I usually work until then. I'll meet you at six-thirty for dinner. Do you want to go on somewhere afterwards? I'll ask my secretary to arrange tickets if you'd like to see a show.'

Ella's gaze flew once more to the selection of bathrobes he kept for his lovers. 'I don't think so,' she said quietly. 'In fact I think it would be better if we kept last night as a one-off. I don't want to have an…an affair with you,' she faltered, flushing when his piercing blue gaze settled thoughtfully on her face. She had the unnerving feeling that he could read the jumble of emotions whirling around her head. 'Neither of us wants to be tied down in a relationship,' she reminded him, despising herself for the way her heart rate quickened when he dropped down onto the bed and wound a few strands of her hair around his fingers.

'I agree,' he said coolly. 'But surely the very fact that we have no desire for a relationship makes us ideal candidates for an affair? There's nothing to stop us being lovers for as long as either one of us wants it to last. And besides,' he murmured, his voice dropping to a deep, sensual tone that caressed her senses, 'one night was not enough for either of us—was it, Ella?'

She gasped when he pushed her flat on her back, but the sound was smothered by his mouth as his head swooped and he claimed her lips in a fierce, hungry kiss that left her in no doubt that one night had not satisfied his desire for her. Last night had not been enough for her either, she thought despairingly. He only had to touch her and molten heat flooded through her veins, and the hot, restless ache in her pelvis made a mockery of her decision to distance herself from him.

Agreeing to an affair with him would only be dangerous if she allowed her emotions to become involved—but she would never do that, she assured herself. She knew what kind of a man he was, and that knowledge made her safe from him—so why not enjoy his sexual expertise? whispered the reckless voice in her head.

When he pushed the sheet down and bent his head to take one dusky pink nipple into his mouth she could not restrain a soft moan, and she arched her back in mute invitation, sliding her hands into his silky black hair to hold him to the task of pleasuring her.

Vadim was tempted, desire corkscrewing through him when he kissed Ella again and felt the tentative foray of her tongue into his mouth. For the first time in his life he was actually contemplating putting pleasure before business. As head of his company, he answered to no one. He could spend all morning making love to Ella and turn up at his office at lunchtime if he pleased. But the realisation that she could exert some sort of hold over him brought his brows together in a slashing frown. No woman had ever caused him to change the way he ran his life. The company he had created from nothing was the most important thing in his life, and women were merely an entertaining distraction from his hectic work schedule—even this woman, he reminded himself fiercely.

Even so, it took all of his formidable willpower to ease the pressure of his lips from the moist softness of hers, and regret tugged in his gut when he lifted his head and sat up. 'Forget going to the theatre; we'll follow dinner with an early night,' he drawled, his mouth curving into an amused smile when colour flared in her cheeks. He watched the confusion in her eyes slowly turn to frustration when she realised that the foreplay was not going to end with another mind-blowing sex session, and he felt a pang of sympathy that, like him, she was going to spend the day in a state of aching arousal. 'But right now you have twenty minutes to get ready, or you'll miss your lift,' he informed her, ignoring her yelp of protest as he flicked back the sheet.

Ella hastily thrust her arms into the robe. 'You think you're God's gift, don't you?' she snapped, incensed by his arrogance, and furious with herself for her shaming inability to resist him. She marched over to the door, but his mocking laughter followed her into the hallway.

'I know I'm the only man who turns you on, angel face. And, more to the point, you know it too,' he said softly.

Vadim's taunt stayed with Ella all day, and for first time in her life she was unable to concentrate on her music—much to the wrath of the RLO's conductor, Gustav, who expected perfection at all times.

'Are you okay?' Jenny asked her during a much-needed break. 'You look pale.'

'I didn't get much sleep last night,' Ella muttered, and then blushed scarlet at the memory of her energetic night with Vadim. Fortunately Jenny seemed not to notice.

'The storm was awful, wasn't it? Why don't you tell Gustav you're feeling unwell and need to go home?'

'No, I can't do that.' Ella shook her head. 'I'd never let the orchestra down, and anyway I need to practise for my solo concert. It's only two weeks away, and I'm already nervous.'

By sheer effort of will she managed to get through the rest of the rehearsal without incurring more of Gustav's sarcasm, but she was dismayed that Vadim had the power to affect the part of her life that she held sacrosanct. Music meant everything to her, and she could not contemplate an affair with him if it would be detrimental to her career. But when she walked out of Cadogan Hall and saw him leaning against his gunmetal grey Aston Martin, the painful jerk of her heart beneath her ribs made a mockery of her determination to play it cool with him.

'Hi,' she greeted him, striving to sound nonchalant.

The amused gleam in his eyes told her he was aware of her internal struggle. He moved with the grace of a big cat, slid his hand beneath her chin and claimed her mouth in a slow, drugging kiss that drove every thought from her mind other than the hot, pulsing need that had been simmering inside her all day. 'How did rehearsals go?'

'Badly,' she muttered tersely, resenting the way one kiss weakened her so that she had to cling to him for support.

His sensual smile stole her breath. 'My day wasn't great either,' he admitted, frowning when he recalled how memories of making love to Ella had interrupted his usually razor-sharp thought processes throughout the day. 'Perhaps we were both distracted by the same fantasies.'

'I don't know what you mean,' she said stiffly.

Vadim laughed and drew her so close against him that she could feel the tantalising hardness of his arousal nudge between her thighs. 'I'll tell you mine, and then you can tell me if yours were the same,' he drawled, and proceeded to whisper the shockingly erotic daydreams that had plagued him, even during an important board meeting, so that Ella's face was scarlet by the time he'd finished.

'Were your thoughts along the same lines?' he queried, his amused smile changing to an expression of sensual hunger when he felt the shiver of desire that ran through her. Ella couldn't answer, her mind still filled with the image of him making love to her across his desk, and with a muttered oath he opened the car door and bundled her inside. 'We'll eat at a little Italian restaurant I know. The food's excellent and, more importantly, the service is quick,' he growled, the sultry gleam in his eyes leaving Ella in no doubt that dinner would be followed by the early night he had promised that morning.

The food at the Trattoria Luciano was as good as Vadim had promised, but Ella barely tasted her chicken *cacciatore*, and, despite having only eaten a couple of apples at lunchtime, her appetite had deserted her. Throughout the meal she could not tear her eyes from Vadim, and although he did better justice to his *lasagne al forno* he did not finish it, and gulped down his glass of red wine before he took her hand and practically dragged her from the restaurant.

He did not say a word on the drive back to Kingfisher House, his tension so tangible that Ella began to think that she had annoyed him in some way. But no sooner had she stepped out of the Aston Martin than he swept her into his arms and strode purposefully into the house.

'You have been on my mind all day,' he admitted harshly as he took the stairs two at a time, shouldered open the door to the bedroom and dropped her onto the bed.

He came down on top of her and captured her mouth in a searing kiss that sent liquid heat flooding through her veins. She was on fire for him instantly, and when she tugged at his shirt buttons and ran her hands over the crisp dark hairs that covered his chest she knew from the erratic thud of his heart that he shared her desperation to experience the tumultuous passion they had shared the previous night.

Her clothes, his, were a barrier he swiftly removed, and he paused only to don protection before he pushed her legs apart and found the moist heat of her femininity with unerring fingers.

'Did you think about me today, Ella?' he growled against her skin, before he closed his lips around the taut peak of her nipple and suckled her until she gasped with pleasure. 'Did you think about this?'

'This' was him sliding one finger and then two deep inside her, and caressing her until she hovered on the edge of ecstasy. 'Yes,' she groaned, knowing that it was pointless to deny it when he could feel the slick wetness of her arousal. During rehearsals she had struggled to concentrate on playing her violin because her mind had insisted on reliving every glorious moment of his lovemaking the previous night. Nothing had ever come between her and her music, and she was dismayed by the level of her fascination with Vadim, but right now nothing mattered except that he should possess her.

'Please…' She gripped his silky dark hair when he lowered his head to her other breast and flicked his tongue across its dusky crest. She hadn't known that she was capable of this level of need, and she held her breath when he positioned himself over her and entered her with a hard, deep thrust that caused her vaginal muscles to convulse around him.

He was her man, and she belonged to him for all time. The words thundered in her head in time with the rhythm of his body as he drove into her again and again, and when he covered her mouth with his she responded to his kiss with an uncontrollable passion that blew his mind.

It couldn't last. His hunger for her was too intense for a leisurely seduction, and he increased his pace, thrusting deeper still and filling her so completely that she arched beneath him and cried out as pleasure crashed over her in a shattering orgasm. The feel of her internal muscles tightening around his shaft was too much for Vadim, and he fought briefly for control, lost it spectacularly, and felt a shudder run through his powerful body as it experienced the sexual release it craved.

Afterwards, when their breathing had finally slowed and he'd rolled off her, she kept her eyes tightly closed, feeling suddenly embarrassed at her wanton response to him.

His rough laughter grazed her skin. 'It's too late to be shy now, angel face. I knew the moment we met that you would be a wildcat in bed,' he added in a satisfied tone. It was the truth, Vadim mused as he swung his legs over the side of the bed and headed for the *en suite* bathroom. That night in Paris he had been shocked by his powerful attraction to Ella, and by the instinctive feeling that they were destined to be lovers. But the idea that she was his woman and his alone was a dangerous one.

He did not want a relationship with her, he reminded himself. Undoubtedly his desire for her would soon pall, and then he would walk away from her—just as he had done with his many previous mistresses. There was no place in his heart for Ella, only in his bed, and the fact that her soft grey eyes and shy smile tugged at his insides was all the more reason to remember the vow he had made after Irina had died, that he would never allow any woman to touch his emotions again.

When Vadim emerged from the bathroom Ella assumed he would rejoin her in bed, but to her disappointment he crossed to the wardrobe, took out jeans and a shirt and proceeded to dress. 'I have to work for a couple of hours,' he explained when he caught her confused expression. 'Why don't you catch up on some sleep? I'll be up later.'

His sensual smile made her heart leap, but she sensed that he had distanced himself from her—or perhaps she had imagined the feeling of closeness between them when he had made love to her? she thought bleakly. What had happened between his walking into the bathroom and returning to the bedroom that had caused him to close up, so that he was once again a brooding stranger? She wished she knew what was going on behind his brilliant blue gaze, but his face was a handsome mask, giving no clue to his thoughts.

Vadim could not have made it clearer that he saw her as his mistress and nothing more. Pride dictated that she should go back to her own flat rather than meekly wait until he wanted to have sex with her again, but he had kept her awake for much of the previous night, and his energetic lovemaking of a few minutes ago had left her exhausted. Her eyelids felt heavy, and within moments she fell into such a deep sleep that she was unaware that Vadim returned to the bedroom less than an hour later and stood by the bed, watching her sleep.

Ella was awoken in the early hours of Saturday morning by Vadim stroking his hands down her body and gently parting her thighs. Any thoughts she might have had of resisting him crumbled, as they had all week, when she saw the sultry gleam in his eyes, and with a sigh she arched her hips to welcome him into her and gave herself up to the exquisite pleasure of his lovemaking.

They spent most of the weekend in bed, or down by the

river, where he made love to her beneath the weeping willow tree whose fragile branches and delicate green leaves provided a private bower. She ached in places she had not known existed, Ella thought ruefully when she woke early on Monday morning and watched the rose-pink glow of dawn spread across the sky. Later today she was flying to Paris to prepare for her solo concert, and she assured herself that the heavy feeling in her stomach was due to nerves about her performance—not because she would be away from Vadim for the next week.

Her planned programme contained several exceptionally complex pieces, particularly the compositions by Paganini, and although she had received intensive coaching from the famous Hungarian violinist Joseph Schranz, she still did not feel confident about the performance. Sleep was impossible when her mind kept running through the pieces, and although it was not yet five a.m. she was desperate to practise. She threw back the sheet, collected her violin from where—much to Vadim's amusement—she kept it beside the bed, and slipped out onto the balcony, closing the door carefully behind her so that she would not disturb him. The morning air was cool and fresh, and the feel of the smooth wood of her violin beneath her fingertips filled Ella with fierce joy. Music meant everything to her, and she was soon lost in her own world, so that when the balcony doors opened she stared at Vadim in confusion.

'Do have any idea what the time is?' he queried mildly, aware of the familiar pull of desire in his groin as he took in her slender figure in the grey silk robe he had bought her because the colour had reminded him of the smoky hue of her eyes. Her pale gold hair streamed around her shoulders, and he could not resist reaching out and winding a long, silky strand around his fingers.

'Um…early,' she mumbled guiltily. 'I'm sorry I woke you,

but the taxi's picking me up at eight to take me to the airport, and I wanted to run through the Paganini compositions one more time.'

His lips twitched. 'I suppose your artistic temperament is to blame for the fact that you've woken before dawn the last couple of days?' He'd felt her increased tension, and had watched her appetite fade to the point that she'd barely eaten a thing at dinner last night. 'Are you always this nervous before a performance?'

'I'm afraid so,' Ella admitted unhappily, embarrassed colour staining her cheeks. She hated the agonising stage fright that gripped her, and had tried various remedies, including hypnotherapy, to try and control it, but she still felt ill with nerves before she gave a solo performance.

'There's no need,' he said gently, surprised by the surge of protectiveness he felt for her. 'You have a phenomenal talent and you play superbly. And if you're leaving at eight, you need to come back to bed now,' he added deeply, drawing her against him and slipping his hand inside her robe to cup her breast in his palm.

'I should get dressed,' Ella murmured, catching her breath when he tugged on her nipple until it swelled and hardened. But he ignored her token protest and scooped her into his arms, capturing her mouth in a hard, hungry kiss as he deposited her on the bed and parted her robe before he positioned himself over her. As he slipped his hand between her legs and gently parted her, his eyes locked with hers, and somehow his intense gaze heightened the intimacy of his caresses, so that she gasped and arched her hips in mute appeal for him to continue his erotic exploration.

'Please...' She clutched his shoulders to urge him down on her, and sighed her pleasure when he entered her with one deep thrust that filled her to the hilt. Nothing mattered but this.

Music, her nervousness about the concert in Paris—everything faded as she surrendered totally to Vadim's mastery.

He was a skilled lover, who knew exactly how to drive her to the edge of ecstasy and keep her teetering there until she begged for the release her body craved while he remained in complete control. But this morning she sensed a difference in him, a new urgency in each powerful thrust as he took her with an almost primitive passion that sent them both swiftly to the heights. Ella could feel the delicious little spasms begin deep within her, and she wrapped her legs around his back to incite him to thrust harder, deeper...

'Vadim...' She could not hold back her desperate plea as the spasms became powerful ripples that radiated out from her central core and engulfed her in mind-blowing pleasure. Frantically she dug her nails into his sweat-sheened shoulders, and felt a surge of feminine triumph when he gave a harsh groan and exploded within her in a shattering climax that left his big body shuddering with after-shocks.

It was ridiculous to feel as though their souls as well as their bodies had joined as one, she told herself when he lay lax on top of her, so that she could feel the thud of his heart gradually return to its normal beat. It was just good sex. But when at last he rolled off her she longed for him to hold her in his arms, and the ache in her heart when he slid out of bed and strolled into the *en suite* bathroom served as a warning sign that she was getting in too deep.

What the hell had happened there? Vadim brooded as he stepped into the shower and began to soap his body. The sex had been good. It was always good with Ella—maybe the best he'd ever had, he admitted. But he'd never lost control like that before. The truth was her passionate response had blown him away, and the knowledge that they would be apart for the next week had intensified his desire, so that it had overwhelmed him and resulted in that spectacular climax. There was no chance he was going to miss her while she was in Paris, he assured himself. They shared fantastic sex, but that was all he wanted from her. Maybe the week apart would lessen his desire for her, and he could end their affair and move on to another pretty blonde.

The Palais Garnier was arguably the most prestigious concert hall in Paris, and with an audience capacity of over two thousand it was the largest venue where Ella had ever given a solo performance.

'It's a full house,' her publicist, Marcus, announced when he bounded into her dressing room. 'Every ticket sold out. I knew we should have arranged for you to perform for two nights rather than just one.' He paused and stared at Ella. 'Heck, you're pale. I'd better call the make-up girl back to see if she can make you look less like a ghost. How do you feel?'

'Sick,' Ella replied truthfully. She bit her lip as panic surged through her. 'I don't think I can go through with it, Marcus.'

'Nonsense,' he told her robustly. 'You always suffer from stage fright, but the minute you start playing you'll be fine. Oh, these came for you,' he added, thrusting the bouquet he was holding into her lap.

Ella despised herself for the way her heart gave a little flip, and she fumbled to open the envelope of the attached card, disappointment swamping her when she read the good luck message from her cousin Stephanie and her family. 'They're lovely,' she murmured as she placed the flowers with the other bouquets she'd received, from her aunt and uncle, and Jenny and her family.

It was stupid to have hoped that Vadim would send her flowers, she told herself impatiently. He'd sent her red roses once, but that was when he had been trying to persuade her into his bed. Now they were lovers—or perhaps sex partners would be a better description of their relationship. She was well aware that she meant nothing to him. He'd probably forgotten about the concert tonight. Maybe he had invited another woman out to dinner while she was away? The mental image of him taking some gorgeous model back to Kingfisher House for the night evoked such searing jealousy inside her that she actually clutched her stomach, as if she had been stabbed with a knife. It shouldn't matter to her if Vadim entertained half a dozen nubile blondes in his bed, she reminded herself, swallowing the bile in her throat and taking a gulp of water, dismayed to see that her hands were shaking.

She couldn't play like this, she thought wildly. Her nervous tension was so acute that it was doubtful she would be able to hold her violin, let alone draw her bow across the strings. She had the career her mother had dreamed of, she reminded herself. But knowing that her adored Mama would have been proud of her did not ease her self-doubt nor lessen her fear at the prospect of walking onto the Palais Garnier's vast stage.

It was ridiculous to feel hurt that Vadim had not contacted her for the whole time she had been in France, and she was ashamed of the tears that stung her eyes. She'd known what she was getting into when she'd agreed to an affair with him—known what kind of man he was—so why did the fact that he had not sent her flowers make her want to bury her head in her hands and weep?

Marcus had gone—presumably to find the make-up girl. But adding some blusher to her cheeks was not going to make her feel any better, Ella thought desperately. In her ivory silk evening dress, with her hair swept up into a chignon, she resembled a wraith rather than a confident woman who was about to walk onto a stage and entertain two thousand people.

With a muttered cry she yanked open the dressing room door—and slammed into the solid wall of a muscular chest.

'Isn't the stage in the other direction?' Vadim enquired lightly. 'Where are you going in such a hurry?' Ella looked like a terrified doe, her eyes huge in her white face. The shimmer of tears on her lashes evoked a curious feeling in his chest, so that without pausing to question what he was doing he drew her into his arms and held her close.

'What are you doing here?' she whispered, clutching his arms as if she feared he was an illusion who would disappear in a puff of smoke.

'Do you think I'd miss a concert by one of the world's most amazing violin virtuosos?' he said softly. 'Also, I wanted to personally deliver these,' he added, lifting a bouquet of fragrant cream roses from the table behind him and handing them to her. 'You didn't think I'd forgotten that this is your big night, did you?'

Utterly overwhelmed, Ella closed her eyes, but could not prevent a single tear from escaping and rolling down her cheek. 'I can't do it,' she said shakily. 'I know I'm going to go to pieces in front of all those people. I must have been mad to think I could ever have a successful career as a soloist when I'm paralysed with nerves before every performance.' She stared at Vadim, half expecting to see mockery in his eyes, but instead she glimpsed an expression of compassion that brought the words tumbling from her mouth. 'This is what my mother wanted for me. She devoted her life to teaching me so that I might have the career she never had. My father was right,' she said miserably. 'He said I was too shy and pathetic to make it as a musician.'

'When did he tell you that?' Vadim asked roughly, feeling again a violent surge of anger at her dead father.

'Oh, he said it every time he tried to persuade me to sell

my violin. It's a Stradivarius and worth a fortune—and my father needed money,' she said bitterly. 'But my mother had left it to me in her will, and he had no claim on it. He was furious when I refused to sell it.' She broke off and bit her lip. 'He never loved me, you know. I don't know why. When I was little I tried so hard to please him—I was desperate for his approval, but I never won it,' she said huskily, unwittingly revealing a vulnerability that tugged at Vadim's insides. The image she presented to the world was of a confident, talented woman on the cusp of an astounding career, but underneath she was still the lonely little girl who had tried to win her father's love and been deeply wounded by his uninterest.

It was little wonder she was afraid of relationships. She had been hurt once, and her determination never to let anyone too close was a self-protective measure to prevent herself from being hurt again. He understood; he'd done the very same thing. The pain of losing his wife and daughter had caused him to build a wall around his heart which he had no intention of ever dismantling. But as he stared down at Ella and watched another tear slip silently down her face, some long-buried emotion inside Vadim stirred into life and he felt a fierce urge to comfort her.

'Your father was wrong,' he said deeply. 'You have a remarkable gift, and you also have an inner strength and grace that will enable you to overcome your nerves. I have absolutely no doubt that you can walk onto the stage tonight and blow the audience away.'

'Do you really think so?' she murmured uncertainly, feeling warmth begin to seep through her veins instead of the icy fear that had frozen her blood. She was suddenly acutely conscious of the muscular strength of his thighs pressing against her, and molten heat unfurled in the pit of her stomach when he slid his hand down to her bottom and pulled her closer still, so that the hard ridge of his arousal nudged between her legs. She lifted her head and drew a sharp breath when she glimpsed the fire blazing in his eyes. After five long, lonely nights away from him her body instantly recognised its master, and when he lowered his head and captured her mouth in a searing kiss she melted against him and wound her arms around his neck, kissing him back with a fervency that drew a low groan from his throat.

Muttering something in Russian, Vadim lifted her up and strode into her dressing room. His sole intention when he had taken her in his arms had been to offer support and encouragement, and hopefully alleviate her stage fright, but Ella was a fever in his blood, and the moment he'd touched her he'd been consumed with the savage need to possess her.

She got to him in a way no other woman ever had, he acknowledged grimly. It was a state of affairs he could not allow to continue, but at this moment he could think of nothing but assuaging the fire that raged in both of them. With shaking fingers he drew the zip of her dress down her spine and slid the narrow straps from her shoulders so that her small, firm breasts spilled into his hands. Her skin felt like satin beneath his lips as he trailed urgent kisses down her throat. He lifted her and sat her on the edge of the dressing table, arching her backwards so that he could close his lips around one dusky nipple and then its twin, sucking each crest until it swelled against his tongue.

Her sharp little breaths matched his own laboured breathing, and their mutual desire blazed out of control, so that he jerked the long skirt of her dress up to her waist and slipped his hand beneath the lacy panel of her knickers to find her slick, wet heat.

At the first stroke of his wickedly inventive fingers Ella sobbed his name, her fears about the concert swept away in the wild torrent of passion. The sexual hunger in Vadim's eyes warned her that he was dangerously out of control, but she loved the fact that his usual formidable restraint had crumbled and his need was a great as hers. With trembling fingers she unfastened his bow tie and wrenched the buttons of his white silk shirt apart. Her nerve faltered momentarily when she fumbled with the zip of his trousers, but when he deftly stepped out of them she dragged his boxers over his hips, and caught her breath when the throbbing length of his erection filled her hands.

'Hold on to me,' he commanded roughly, and she immediately clung to his broad, bronzed shoulders as he slipped his hands beneath her bottom, lifted her, and sank his swollen shaft into her with a hard thrust that drove the breath from her body.

She was dimly aware of a crash as the various jars of toiletries on the dressing table fell to the floor. Thank heaven he'd locked the door, was her last coherent thought, before she caught and matched his pagan rhythm and tilted her hips to meet each devastating thrust. Harder, faster—this was sex at its most primitive, and she gloried in the power of it, her whole being focused on reaching that magical place that was uniquely special to them. It couldn't last. She felt him tense and knew he was fighting for control, but as her body arched with the drenching pleasure of her orgasm she heard the ragged groan that was torn from his throat and felt the judders that ripped through him as he exploded in a violent climax and spilled into her.

Ella slowly came back to earth to face the realisation that they had just had wild sex on her dressing table, and that she was due to perform in front of two thousand people in ten minutes' time. Usually she would be sick with nerves by now, she thought ruefully. But Vadim had commanded her mind as well as her body, and she was still too dazed with pleasure to worry about the concert.

'You'll have to make love to me before every performance,' she quipped huskily, blushing when she saw the marks on his chest where she had raked him with her nails.

The flare of colour on her cheeks evoked a curious ache in Vadim's chest. Beneath her shy exterior she was a tigress, but he was the only man to have discovered her sensual nature and he was startled by the possessive feeling that surged through him. 'I missed you,' he admitted roughly, noting how her eyes had darkened with an emotion he did not want to define.

The moment was broken by the sound of Marcus Benning's voice from the other side of the door.

'Ella—time to go. Are you ready?'

'Almost.' A bubble of laughter rose in her throat as Vadim swiftly donned his trousers while she refastened his shirt buttons. He slid the straps of her dress back into place, set her on her feet and grimaced as he smoothed the creases out of her skirt.

'At least you've got more colour in your cheeks,' he murmured, running his finger lightly down her flushed face. 'How are the nerves?'

'What nerves?' Her smile stole his breath. She picked up her violin and headed for the door. 'Wish me luck?'

'You don't need it, angel face. You'll wow the audience.' His eyes held hers. 'Play for me,' he said softly.

'I will.' She took a deep breath before she unlocked the door, and smiled serenely at Marcus as she swept past him and along the corridor towards the stage.

CHAPTER NINE

SHE received a standing ovation. Blinking bemusedly in the glare of the lights, Ella gave a final bow and turned to walk off the stage, the thunderous applause from the audience echoing in her ears.

'You were bloody marvellous,' Marcus greeted her buoyantly. 'I knew your nerves would disappear the minute you played the first note.'

Ella nodded weakly. She felt utterly drained, both emotionally and physically, and longed to retreat to the quiet of her dressing room, but she knew that Marcus had arranged for her to give interviews to several journalists at the after-concert party.

She spent the next hour chatting and smiling until her jaw ached. Marcus paraded her around the reception, where it seemed that everyone wanted to meet her, but although she scanned the room whenever she had the opportunity she was disappointed not to see Vadim. Perhaps he had flown back to London immediately after the concert? She knew he was negotiating an important deal in the capital, and the fact that he owned a private jet meant that he could travel whenever it suited him.

Taking advantage of a lull in conversation, she escaped to a quiet corner of the room and rubbed her brow wearily, aware of the familiar throbbing pain behind her temples that warned of the onset of a migraine.

'Do you have your painkillers with you?' Vadim materialised at her side, and she was so shocked at the sight of him, when she had convinced herself he had returned to England, that for a few seconds she could not disguise the emotion that flared in her eyes.

He was so stunningly handsome that she actually hurt inside when she looked at him, but she did not possess sufficient willpower to look away. They were back in Paris, where they had first met. She recalled vividly the feeling that she'd been struck by a lightning bolt when she had glanced across a crowded room and seen him for the first time. She had known then that he spelled trouble, she mused ruefully. She had sensed that he would be dangerous to her peace of mind and she had tried to fight the simmering sexual chemistry between them. But the truth was he fascinated her in a way no other man had ever done.

He had stated that their affair would last until either of them wanted to end it. But as her eyes locked with his brilliant blue gaze a sense of longing for something she could not explain unfurled deep inside her, and with it came a sharp stab of pain as she envisaged a time in the probably not too distant future when they would no longer be lovers. She could not be falling for him, she reassured herself frantically. She always felt emotional after a performance, and the ache in her heart was definitely not because she wished for more from her relationship with Vadim than simply great sex.

Vadim watched the play of emotions in Ella's stormy grey eyes and correctly deciphered each one. He frowned, silently debating whether it would be fair to go ahead with his plans. He did not want to hurt her. But, reasoned the voice in his head, he had made it clear from the beginning that he had no intention of allowing their affair to develop into something deeper.

He'd only ever wanted a mutually enjoyable sexual liaison, and he was infuriated that she seemed to have some sort of hold over him. He had spoken the truth when he'd told her that he had missed her during the five days—and hellish nights—that she had been in Paris, preparing for the concert. But he knew from experience that, for him, prolonged intimacy bred boredom. The best way to get her out of his system was to spend all his time with her, and that was exactly what he was going to do for the next days or weeks—however long it took for him to tire of her.

'My tablets are in my dressing room,' she told him. 'Do you think anyone will notice if I disappear from the party for a while?'

'I've already told Marcus we're leaving.' Vadim smiled at her startled expression and slipped his arm around her waist to steer her over to the door. 'I assume you've had enough of the party?'

'Heavens, yes,' she agreed fervently. 'I'm staying at the Intercontinental again. Have you booked into a hotel?' she queried when they reached her dressing room. She quickly took a couple of the strong painkillers that would hopefully prevent her headache from developing into a full-blown migraine.

'No, I'm flying out on the jet tonight—and you're coming with me.'

Ella's heart flipped at the prospect of returning to Kingfisher House with Vadim when she had expected to spend another night at her hotel, alone.

'I take it you have no argument with the arrangements?' he murmured as he drew her into his arms.

'None at all. I can't wait to go home,' she admitted, hectic colour staining her cheeks when she imagined him making love to her in his big bed back at the house she loved. 'But I'll have to stop off at the hotel to collect my things.'

'One of my staff will do that.' He claimed her mouth in a long, sensual kiss that stirred her desire back into urgent life, and when he finally released her she snatched up her handbag and followed him out to the corridor. She collected her violin from the security desk—after refusing point-blank Vadim's suggestion that his PA would arrange for its safe transportation.

'My violin stays with me at all times,' she explained.

'So I've discovered. I must admit it's a novelty to share my bedroom with a musical instrument,' Vadim said dryly, referring to her insistence on keeping her violin beside the bed at Kingfisher House.

They emerged from the Palais Garnier to be met by a barrage of flashing camera bulbs. Ella had known that her performance had attracted some media interest, but it soon became clear that the press were more curious about her relationship with playboy billionaire Vadim Aleksandrov. 'Maybe I should go back inside,' she muttered as they were jostled by the dozens of photographers who were vying to snap the best shots of the enigmatic Russian and his beautiful companion who was rapidly becoming an international star.

In reply Vadim slid his arm around her waist and shouldered his way through the crowd, seemingly unconcerned that his action had incited fevered interest among the journalists. 'Don't worry about them,' he told her when they finally reached the car, where his chauffeur was holding the door open for them to scramble inside.

'But they'll think we're…together,' Ella said uncertainly, holding up a hand to shield her eyes from the glare of the camera bulbs that continued to flash outside the car's windows. 'You know how the paparazzi exaggerate things. News that we're having a torrid affair will probably be in all tomorrow's tabloids.'

Vadim shrugged. 'What does is matter what they say? It's the truth, anyway. For now, we *are* together, angel face.'

He seemed perfectly at ease with the likelihood that their affair would soon be common knowledge, but in London Ella had noted that he had deliberately avoided places where they might have been spotted by the press, and had taken her to out-of-the-way restaurants where they had not attracted attention. Did the fact that he now seemed happy for them to be seen in public together mean that he wanted their relationship to develop into something deeper than a meaningless sexual liaison? she wondered, annoyed with herself for the little flutter of hope in her chest. Daydreams were for children, she reminded herself irritably. And since when had she decided that Vadim was her knight in shinning armour?

They took off from Charles de Gaulle Airport within minutes of boarding the Learjet. Ella had never been on a private plane before, and as she glanced around at the elegant cabin, with its cream leather sofas, cocktail bar and vast cinema screen, she appreciated for the first time how very different Vadim's world was from hers. Even the two female flight attendants looked like top models, she noted wryly, and a poisonous little voice in her head wondered if they provided in-flight entertainment when he travelled on his numerous business trips around the world.

'You look like a ghost,' Vadim murmured, frowning as he studied her pale features. 'Is your headache worse?'

'No, I'm just tired,' she replied quickly, praying that his uncanny ability to read her mind would not reveal the flare of jealousy that had ripped through her when one of the flight attendants had leaned unnecessarily close to him as she had served him his drink. 'Where are we going?' she queried in a puzzled voice, when he unfastened her seat belt and drew her to her feet.'

'Bed,' he informed her succinctly.

Her heart lurched at the wicked gleam in his eyes, and she

gasped when he swung her into his arms and strode towards the back of the plane. He shouldered a door and walked into a plush sleeping compartment, complete with vast double bed. 'You certainly like to travel in comfort,' she muttered as he laid her down and removed her shoes. The idea that he was going to make love to her when they were thirty thousand feet in the air was shockingly exciting, but to her dismay he did not join her on the bed, instead drawing the cover up to her chin as if he were taking care of a small child.

'Go to sleep,' he bade her gently, wondering why her air of fragility tugged on his heart. 'I'll wake you when we're about to land in Nice.'

The moment Ella's head touched the pillows exhaustion overwhelmed her, and her sleepy brain could not comprehend Vadim's last statement. 'Don't you mean Heathrow?' she mumbled. 'We're flying to London, not Nice.'

'Actually, we're on our way to my villa in the Cap d'Antibes,' he informed her, pushing her gently back down on the mattress when she struggled to sit up. 'Nice is the closest airport.'

She shook her head in confusion. 'Do you mean we're going to France for the weekend?'

'I'm planning on us staying for a few weeks,' he informed her smoothly.

'Well, that might be your plan, but it's certainly not mine,' she snapped, annoyed by the arrogance in his tone. 'I can't just disappear to France indefinitely.'

'I checked with Marcus Benning, who told me your diary is clear for the next month. You're not scheduled to record the film score with the RLO until the end of August. Marcus actually agreed with me that it will do you good to have a holiday.'

'Oh, did he? It's nice to know the two of you have orga-nised my life for me,' Ella said tightly, using sarcasm to disguise her panic at the prospect of spending the next few weeks with Vadim at his villa. He had changed the rules of their affair without asking her, she thought bitterly. Sharing a holiday with him and being with him twenty-four hours a day was a daunting prospect. They might drive each other mad. But far more worrying was the possibility that she would fall even deeper under his spell—and that would be just asking to have her heart broken.

She could see from the determined set of Vadim's jaw that arguing about the trip to his villa would be pointless, especially as they were already *en route* to France. But she would be on her guard against him, she assured herself as she lay back down on the pillows. And with that thought firmly in her mind she fell asleep.

The Villa Corraline was a stunning Provençal-style house, set in beautiful grounds and commanding spectacular views of the coastline of the Côte d'Azur. It was dark when they arrived, and Ella was instantly captivated by the sight of the house, lit with lamps which turned the pink walls to a deep coral colour. When she followed Vadim inside, she glimpsed various elegant, marble-floored rooms, but she was still dazed with sleep, and only made a token protest when he swept her into his arms and carried her up the sweeping staircase to the huge, circular master bedroom, which was dominated by an enormous bed.

'I only packed enough clothes for a week,' she said, when she caught sight of the small suitcase that a member of Vadim's staff must have collected from her hotel in Paris.

'You'll find everything you need in here,' he replied, pulling open one of the wardrobes to reveal a rail full of dresses and skirts in a rainbow of soft colours that would suit Ella's delicate skin-tone.

Frowning, she ran her hand along the row of clothes, noting that each item carried the label of a top design house. 'I don't understand. Who do these things belong to?' she asked, a sinking feeling in her stomach as she remembered how he kept a selection of bathrobes in his wardrobe at Kingfisher House for his lovers. If he thought she would wear clothes belonging to one of his previous mistresses, he'd better think again!

'They're yours. I gave details of your size and colouring to a personal stylist and asked her to put together a selection of outfits for you,' he explained with a shrug—as if the subject of what she would wear during their stay in France was of minimal interest.

'I can't possibly allow you to buy clothes for me,' Ella told him fiercely. She owned a few designer evening gowns which she had bought for performances, and she had a good idea how much each item hanging in the wardrobe must have cost. The idea of being beholden to any man was repugnant to her. 'I pay my own way,' she told Vadim stiffly. 'Perhaps your *personal stylist* will be able to take the clothes back and get a refund.'

Ella was the only woman he had met since he had achieved billionaire status who did not seem to think that an affair with him included unrestricted use of his credit card, Vadim noted.

His eyes narrowed on her flushed face, and for a moment Ella thought she had angered him, but then his mouth curved into a sensual smile that she found impossible to resist. 'Don't be ridiculous. You need something to wear while you're here. Many of my friends own houses along the coast, and we will do a fair amount of socialising. Although if you insist on walking around naked for the next couple of weeks I won't complain,' he promised, in a voice that was suddenly as rich and sensuous as crushed velvet.

The brush of his mouth across her lips, before he trailed a line of kisses down her throat to the pulse beating jerkily at its base, demolished her thought processes and effectively put an end to further argument about the clothes he'd bought for her. But later that night, after Ella had briefly donned a sexy black silk chemise, and he had teased and tormented her senses as he had taken his time removing it, she made a silent vow that she would only wear the clothes while she was his mistress, and would return them when their affair was over.

After a night when Vadim made love to her three times, and drove her to a shattering climax on each occasion, Ella did not stir until mid-morning. Sunlight dancing across her face finally prompted her to open her eyes, and she caught her breath at the magnificent view of the cobalt-blue Mediterranean visible through the glass walls of the circular room.

'I take it the house meets with your approval?' Vadim was propped up on one elbow beside her, amusement gleaming in his eyes when he took in her rapt expression. He looked devastatingly sexy, with a night's growth of dark stubble shading his jaw and his olive-gold skin gleaming in the sunlight, and the sheet lying low over his hips barely covered the jutting length of his arousal.

'It's wonderful.' Looking at him made her heart ache, and she quickly glanced back at the view, praying he would never guess how much he affected her.

'You haven't seen the pool yet—or the gardens, or the private beach.' Her beautiful smile tugged at Vadim's insides. Her excitement was infectious, and for the first time in years he found he was looking forward to having some time away from the punishing work schedule he imposed on himself. 'We'll spend the day exploring the house and grounds,' he promised, 'and this afternoon we can go to the beach and I'll take you out on the jet-ski.'

They quickly fell into a pattern of spending their days by

the pool or on the beach, sometimes driving into Antibes town, or along the coast to Cannes and St Raphael. Occasionally Vadim retreated to his study to work during the afternoons, but more often he sat on the terrace and listened to Ella play the violin for two or three hours at a stretch.

'What are you going to serenade me with today?' he quipped late one afternoon, when they had retreated from the blazing heat of the patio to the shade of the tall pine trees that surrounded the garden.

'I thought a little Tchaikovsky to start with, followed by Brahms.' Ella turned the pages of her music score and settled her violin beneath her chin. 'I still find it strange to play wearing a bikini,' she owned with a smile.

'You could always take the bikini off,' Vadim suggested dulcetly, 'if that will help?'

She blushed at the wicked gleam in his eyes. 'I don't think that's a good idea. You know what happens when I take my clothes off.'

'Mmm, I feel duty-bound to make love to you.' Vadim trailed his eyes over Ella's slender figure in her minuscule turquoise bikini, and allowed his gaze to linger on her small, firm breasts which were barely covered by the triangles of material. Would he ever have enough of her? he wondered as he felt himself harden. She was like a fever in his blood, and he was tempted to carry her inside and sate his hunger for her for the third time that day.

'I really need to practise,' she murmured, recognising the sultry intent in his eyes.

His smile stole Ella's breath, and her heart seemed to swell in her chest until she was sure he could see it beating frantically beneath her ribs. Surely she was not imagining the close bond that she sensed was developing between them? she thought, hope soaring inside her. They had become friends as well as lovers, Vadim shared her love of music, and he was the only person she had ever met apart from her mother who seemed to understand how much it meant to her.

'Then play for me,' he bade her, leaning back on the sun lounger and folding his arms beneath his head. 'I'll conserve my energy for later.'

For the next hour Ella was utterly absorbed in her music, but at last she lowered her bow and flexed her fingers. Vadim was no longer watching her play, and instead was staring across the garden to the sea, which sparkled like a sapphire beneath the dense blue sky.

'Penny for them?' she said cheerfully, her teasing smile fading when she glimpsed an expression of raw pain in his eyes, before his urbane mask slipped back into place. 'Is—is something troubling you, Vadim?' she faltered, so shaken by what she had seen that she ignored his warning frown that he did not welcome questions about his personal life. It was not the first time she had sensed that his thoughts were far away, and when he stared at her without replying she found his brooding silence unnerving.

He shrugged laconically. 'What could be troubling me, angel face?' he drawled. 'I'm enjoying good weather, fine food and the company of a beautiful mistress in my bed every night. What more could any man ask for?'

Mistress! How she hated that word, Ella thought savagely, looking away from him so that he would not see how much his casual description of her role in his life had hurt her. Vadim was a charming and charismatic companion, and a generous lover, but she sensed that there were secrets in his past that he would never reveal to her.

'I just thought you looked bothered by something,' she muttered stiffly, telling herself that it was ridiculous to feel rejected just because he chose not to confide in her. They did not have that kind of relationship, she reminded herself. She was his temporary mistress, and all the wishing in the world would not change the situation.

'It's sweet of you to be concerned about me,' he said, in a faintly amused tone that caused a flush of embarrassment to stain her cheeks. 'But I assure you there is no need.' Vadim's conscience gnawed at him when he saw the flare of hurt in her eyes. He knew he had sounded abrupt, but he had no intention of revealing to Ella that her rendition of Mozart's exquisite *Eine Kleine Nachtmusik* had reminded him of an evening many years ago, when he had taken Irina to a concert by the Moscow State Symphony.

It had been a few months after their marriage, a celebration of the news that Irina was pregnant with their first child, and he could still recall the excitement he had felt that he was going to be a father. Why had he allowed his ambition to make money to become more important than his wife and child? he wondered bleakly. His obsession with developing his business had hurt Irina, but by the time he had realised just how much she and Klara meant to him they had already made their fateful journey to Irina's home village, and although he had followed them he had arrived too late to save them.

'Did you remember we're meeting Sergey and Lena Tarasov for dinner tonight?' He dragged his mind from the past and forced a casual tone.

'I hadn't forgotten.' Ella glanced at her watch. 'I think I'll go and shower and start getting ready now,' she muttered, needing to get away from him before she gave in to the stupid urge to burst into tears.

She had met Vadim's Russian friends the Tarasovs on several occasions. They were a charming couple, and she enjoyed their company, but if she was honest she would have preferred an intimate dinner on the terrace with Vadim, followed by a stroll along the beach in the moonlight before he swept her off to bed. When they had first arrived in Antibes they had spent many evenings alone together at the villa, but lately he had accepted invitations to social events every night, and she wondered if it was a sign that he was growing bored of her.

She'd known right from the start that their relationship would only ever be a temporary affair, she reminded herself when she stepped out of the shower, smoothed fragrant lotion onto her lightly tanned skin and returned to the bedroom to dress. She had also known that falling in love with him would be emotional suicide—but Vadim had dismantled her defences one by one, until she feared she was in danger of losing her heart to him irrevocably.

A noise from the doorway alerted her to his presence, and she pinned a smile to her face as she spun round and swept a hand over her dress. 'What do you think?'

'I think you look stunning,' Vadim said truthfully, feeling the familiar tug of sexual hunger in his groin when he studied her. The black silk strapless sheath was deceptively simple, its bodice cut low over the upper curves of her breasts, and the side split in the skirt revealing a glimpse of slender thigh encased in gossamer-fine black hose.

With her hair swept up into a chignon, she looked elegant and desirable—the perfect attributes for a mistress. She would turn heads tonight, and he knew that other men would fantasise about her slender body beneath her dress and envy him. But she belonged to him, and only him. He was surprised by the feeling of possessiveness that surged through him. She meant nothing to him, he reminded himself grimly. She was just another blonde, passing briefly through his life, and the realisation that he was becoming addicted to her company—in and out of the bedroom—was the reason he had started to accept social invitations which ensured that he spent less time alone with her.

'I have a present for you,' he said, strolling over to her and taking a slim black velvet box from his pocket.

Ella caught her breath when he extracted a glittering diamond necklace from the box and fastened it around her throat. 'I can't possibly accept it,' she faltered as she stared at her reflection in the mirror and watched how the diamonds sparkled in the golden glow of the setting sun. 'It must be worth a fortune.'

He shrugged. 'You deserve it.' Unlike his previous mistresses, Ella never expected him to lavish her with gifts. 'It pleases me to buy things for you. Don't you like it?' he murmured, his voice whispering against her skin as he traced his lips up her neck and found the sensitive spot below her ear.

'It's beautiful.' Ella said quietly, but the words 'you deserve it' echoed in her mind. Did he regard the necklace as payment for her services in the bedroom—along with the designer clothes he had bought her? She was his mistress, she reminded herself dully, and he was a billionaire who probably bought all his mistresses diamonds. She remembered the daisy chain he had made for her the previous day, when they had lain on the grass beneath the shade of the olive trees, and wondered what he would say if she told him she would rather wear the simple necklace made of flowers that was now hidden in her bedside drawer than the priceless and meaningless precious gems that felt like a weight around her neck.

Vadim's Aston Martin had been shipped to the villa a few days after their arrival. The powerful car ate up the twenty miles between Antibes and Monaco, and they drove through the Principality to the famous Grand Casino, where they met up with the Tarasovs.

'It's a spectacular place, isn't it?' Lena Tarasov murmured, after the two couples had dined in the exclusive restaurant and were strolling through the casino's opulent gaming rooms, where magnificent crystal chandeliers sparkled down on the array of glittering diamonds and gems worn by every designer-clad female guest. 'Monte Carlo is a world away from the slums of Moscow, where Sergey, Vadim and I grew up.'

Ella glanced at the beautiful dark-haired Russian woman at her side. 'Did you know Vadim when he was a child?' she asked curiously.

'No, he and Sergey became friends when they were in the army, and Vadim was best man at our wedding. When Sergey's electronics company folded a few years ago, Vadim offered him the position of company director at his Russian headquarters.' Lena smiled. 'Vadim is a good man and loyal friend. To be honest I think he was glad of the opportunity to hand over the Russian operation to someone he knew he could trust and move to Europe. Russia holds bad memories for him.'

Ella nodded, recalling Vadim's description of his unhappy childhood with his father and cruel grandmother, after his mother had abandoned him. 'Yes, he's told me about his family.'

'He has?' Lena gave her a speculative glance. 'I had not realised. As far as I know, Vadim has never spoken about his wife and daughter to anyone but his closest friends.' She appeared unaware of the shock wave that had ripped through Ella, and gave her another warm smile. 'Losing them both was such a terrible tragedy. I don't think Vadim has ever really come to terms with it. He has always maintained he would never fall in love again. But...' She shrugged her shoulders expressively. 'You are different to all his other women. I said so to Sergey the first time we met you. Maybe you can unlock Vadim's heart and make his eyes smile again?'

They had reached the salon, where the two men were already seated at the roulette table. The room was hot and busy, and buzzing with the hubbub of conversation, and Ella struggled to squeeze through the crowds thronged around the tables, trying to keep up with Lena so that she could question the Russian woman about her astounding revelation that Vadim—the most commitment-phobic playboy on the planet—had once had a wife and child.

She felt numb with shock. He'd never said a word to her in all the time they had spent together. But of course he did not regard her as one of his closest friends, she thought bitterly. She was just his temporary mistress, and he kept her shut out of his life. Contrary to what Lena thought, she certainly did not have the key to his heart.

CHAPTER TEN

'YOU'RE very quiet tonight. What's the matter?' Vadim queried as the Aston Martin sped along the road back to Antibes.

Ella shot him a lightning glance and felt her heart contract at the sight of his hard, classically sculpted features highlighted by the moonlight. 'I've got a headache. I'll take a couple of migraine tablets when we get back.' She turned away from him and stared out of the window, wondering why misery had settled like a lead weight in her stomach. What did it matter if he had been married and had had a child? His past had nothing to do with her. But during their time in Antibes she had felt closer to him than she ever had to any other human being, and, fool that she was, she had kidded herself that he was beginning to regard her as more than a convenient sex partner. The discovery that he had deliberately withheld important details about his past made a mockery of her stupid daydream that he would ever want a meaningful relationship with her.

'I have to make a call to the US,' he told her when they entered the Villa Corraline, and immediately headed for his study. 'Why don't you go up to bed? You look all in.'

As soon as she reached the bedroom, Ella stripped out of her evening dress and took off the diamond necklace. Maybe she was oversensitive, but all evening she'd felt as though the glittering gems had screamed the fact that she was Vadim's mistress, and she had been aware of speculative glances from various predatory women, clearly wondering how long she would hold on to her position.

Recalling that Vadim had dropped the velvet box that had contained the necklace into his bedside cabinet, she crossed to his side of the bed, opened the drawer and deposited the diamonds. She was about to shut the drawer again when something caught her attention.

The rag-doll was clearly old, and cheaply made. Someone had repaired the stitching on the arms and legs with a slightly darker thread, and some of the stuffing must have escaped because the doll was limp and strangely misshapen. Carefully, Ella took the doll from the drawer. Beneath it were two photographs: one of a woman with a mass of brown hair, holding a baby in her arms, the other depicting a little girl of maybe four or five, with an impish smile and a mop of blonde curls. The photos were not of particularly good quality and were curled at the edges, as if they had been held many times. They could only be of Vadim's wife and child, she realised, her heart thumping as she stared at them in fascination, unaware of the faint sound of footfall until he materialised in front of her.

Flushing guiltily, she quickly dropped the photographs into her lap. 'I'm sorry. I didn't mean to pry,' she mumbled. 'I was putting the necklace away when I saw the pictures…and I was curious.' Vadim's silence was unnerving; the expression on his hard face unreadable, and her hands shook slightly as she handed the doll and photos to him. 'Cute little girl,' she commented, striving to sound normal as she got up from the bed.

'Yes.' He finally spoke, and gave a faint shrug of his shoulders, his eyes veering from her face to the pictures. 'They're friends—in Russia.'

Ella nodded. 'I see.' She picked up her robe and headed

swiftly for the *en suite* bathroom. She was not one of Vadim's closest friends; she was the woman he had sex with. There was no reason why he would confide in her, she reminded herself.

In the bathroom she removed her make-up, washed her face and released the pins from her chignon, pulling the brush through her hair with automatic strokes until she could not put off returning to the bedroom any longer. Thank God she'd made the excuse about having a headache earlier, she thought bleakly. She knew she was being stupid, but she could not bear to make love with Vadim tonight, when his lie about the identities of the woman and child in the photographs emphasised how unimportant she was to him.

He had switched off the lamps so that the room was shadowed; fingers of silvery moonlight were glimmering through the windows. Vadim had stepped outside onto the terrace. She could see him sitting on the garden bench, his shoulders slumped in an air of such utter loneliness that instead of sliding into bed she was drawn towards the open doors, her grey silk gown rustling as she hurried down the steps.

He looked up as she approached, and she caught her breath at the expression of haunted agony on his face.

'The woman in the photo was my wife,' he said harshly.

Ella's eyes flew to the photographs in his hands, and her heart contracted when she saw him stroke his finger lightly over the face of the little girl.

'And this was my daughter—Klara.' The silence trembled between them before he added in a tightly controlled voice, 'They're both dead.'

He passed his hand over his eyes, and the betraying gesture tore Ella's heart to shreds. She was stunned to see this powerful man suddenly so vulnerable. She wanted to go to him, hold him, but fear that he would reject her sympathy held her immobile.

'I'm so sorry.' She didn't know what to say, and the words

seemed desperately inadequate. When Lena Tarasov had revealed that Vadim had been married, she had been bitterly hurt that he had never spoken about his past to her. But now, as she witnessed his raw pain, she hated herself for having been so childish. He had clearly been devastated by the loss of his wife and daughter, and who could blame him if he found it hard to talk about their deaths?

'What…what happened?' she asked huskily.

His throat worked, and his lashes were spiked with moisture when he lifted his head and met her startled gaze. 'They were killed in an avalanche which hit Irina's parents' village,' he explained harshly. 'Most of Rumsk was wiped out.' He stared down at the photos in his hand. 'My parents-in-law lived on the lower slopes of the mountain, and when hundreds of tons of snow hurtled down the mountainside no one in the house stood a chance. It was three days before the rescue team found Irina, and another two before they reached Klara.' His voice cracked with emotion. 'Of course it was too late. When they found Klara she was still holding her doll.'

He picked up the rag-doll and swallowed the constriction in his throat. He could sense Ella's shock, and knew she was struggling for something to say. But there was nothing to be said. Irina and Klara were gone, and no amount of words would bring them back.

Ella's throat ached with tears, but she forced herself to speak. 'When?' she whispered.

'Ten years ago.' His mouth twisted into a grimace. 'Today would have been Klara's fifteenth birthday.' The memories had been agonising today, but he had suppressed his pain in the same way that he always did, and had arranged to social-ise with friends to prevent himself from dwelling on the past. But now the evening was over, and he could no longer banish the images in his head of his angelic-faced little girl.

'I suppose your…wife…' Ella stumbled slightly over the word '…had taken your daughter to visit her parents.' She fell silent, finding it impossible to imagine how terrible it must have been for Vadim when he'd heard news of the disaster.

Vadim stared silently across the dark garden, reliving those harrowing hours and days when he had joined the search teams and dug through the snow until his shoulder muscles had burned with his frantic efforts to find Klara, so that he could place her body with Irina's in the mortuary. Even after ten years, the memory of finding his lifeless daughter still ripped his heart out.

He didn't understand why he suddenly felt an overwhelming urge to confide in Ella. All he knew was that somehow she had crept beneath his guard, so that for the first time in a decade he found himself contemplating a relationship that encompassed more than mindless sex.

Ella looked ethereal and achingly fragile, with her silvergrey gown fluttering gently in the breeze and her pale gold hair streaming like a river of silk down her back. But her loveliness was more than skin-deep. He had discovered that she was funny, witty, fiercely intelligent, and she possessed a depth of compassion that he had never found in any other woman. He admired her strength of will as she fought her nerves to pursue her career as a soloist, and he recognised the vulnerability she tried so hard to disguise. She needed—deserved—more than he could give her. He had failed in one relationship, and that failure had resulted in unimaginable pain. He could never risk failing again.

'If you want the truth, Irina was in Rumsk because she had walked out on our marriage,' he told her savagely, the familiar feeling of self-loathing rushing over him. 'I had been away on yet another business trip, and on my return I found a note from her explaining that she felt I didn't love her, and that she was taking Klara to stay with her parents. I knew Irina had been upset that I spent so much time at work,' he admitted heavily. 'I was determined to reassure her that she and Klara were more important to me than anything, and I raced after them, but I reached Rumsk after the avalanche had hit.'

'Oh, Vadim.' It was a cry from the heart, torn from Ella when she glimpsed the agony in his eyes. There was no thought in her head to judge him. She flew across the terrace, uncaring that she was in danger of revealing how she felt about him, intent only on trying to comfort him.

He had risen to his feet, and stiffened when she flung her arms around his waist. 'You have to understand I was not a good husband,' he said roughly. 'I was obsessed with work and establishing my company, and I did not spend enough time at home—even when Irina pleaded with me to devote more time to her and Klara.' His jaw tightened as he fought to control the emotions surging through him. 'Irina accused me of not loving her. She was wrong; I did love her—but I didn't value what I had until she had left me, and she and Klara were killed before I had the chance to tell them both what they meant to me.' He drew a ragged breath. 'I should not have married. I was selfish and driven by my determination to succeed. I put my interests first, and in that respect perhaps I am not so dissimilar to your father,' he finished grimly.

'You are nothing like my father.' Ella fiercely refuted the suggestion. When she had first met Vadim she *had* believed he was a man like her father, a heartless playboy who only cared about himself. But since they had become lovers he had treated her with kindness and respect, as if he valued her as a person and did not regard her merely as a form of entertainment in his bed.

But thoughts like those were dangerous, she conceded bleakly. Vadim might have a depth to him that she would not have believed in the early days of their relationship, but he had made it clear that an affair was all he would ever want from her. Lena Tarasov had stated that he would never fall in love again, and now she knew why. He was still in love with his dead wife, and consumed with guilt that he had somehow failed Irina and his little daughter. Falling in love with him would be emotional suicide, warned a voice in her head. But in her heart she knew the warning was too late. She loved him, and learning about the tragedy of his past made her love him more.

'The avalanche that killed Irina and Klara was a terrible accident, but you were not to blame for their deaths,' she told him gently. 'You say you feel guilty that you devoted all your time to your business, but I imagine your determination to succeed was so that you could give your wife and daughter a better life.'

'I wanted to buy a house with a garden for Klara to play in—give her the things I'd never had as a child.' He gave a grim smile. 'She loved music, and wanted to learn to play an instrument, but it was impossible in our cramped apartment.' He shook his head. 'Ironically, most of the children from the village survived. They had gone on a school trip and returned to find their school buried and many of their parents dead. I set up an orphanage and paid to have the village rebuilt, but no amount of money can rebuild shattered lives. I go back every year, but the new Rumsk is a strangely quiet place, shrouded in sadness.'

He expelled a ragged breath and gave in to the temptation to slide his arms around Ella's waist and hold her close. Her hair smelled of lemons, and he could feel the thud of her heart beneath her ribs, its steady beat strangely comforting. He turned his head and felt a curious tugging sensation in his chest when she brushed her lips over his cheek, his jaw, and finally across his mouth, in a feather-light caress that soothed his ravaged soul.

He needed her tonight; he needed her in a way he had never needed any woman—although he refused to assimilate the emotions churning inside him. Her mouth moved over his in a tentative kiss that made his stomach muscles clench, desire and some other indefinable feeling surging through him, so that with a groan he swept her up into his arms and strode back across the terrace.

She was the most generous lover he had ever known, and the sweetness of her response when he laid her on the bed and claimed her mouth with his evoked an ache around his heart. He knew every inch of her body, but he revelled in exploring every dip and curve again as he opened her robe and stroked his hands over her satin-soft skin. Her firm breasts filled his palms, and he heard her swiftly indrawn breath when he bent his head and closed his lips around her nipple, laving it with his tongue until she clutched his shoulders and twisted her hips in a mute plea for him to slide his hand between her legs.

Ella gasped at the first brush of his thumb across the ultra-sensitive nub of her clitoris, and molten heat pooled between her thighs as her body prepared for Vadim's possession. He gently parted her, slid a finger in deep to work his magic, and in response she traced her hand through the crisp dark hairs that arrowed down to his hips. She heard his low groan as she caressed the throbbing length of his arousal.

She loved him, and tonight she sensed that he needed to lose himself in the passion that, as always, had swiftly built between them. When he moved over her she arched her hips to meet him, and held his gaze as he entered her with one deep thrust that joined their bodies as one. He was haunted by his past, but if he was able to forget the pain of his loss in these moments when they soared to the heights of sexual pleasure then she was glad, and she matched his rhythm, urging him to find solace in the explosive ecstasy of their mutual climax and holding him close against her heart when they slowly came back down to earth.

For long moments afterwards he lay lax on top of her, his face buried in her throat. Ella's heart contracted when she felt wetness on her skin, and with shaking fingers she touched his cheek, wanting to weep at the evidence of his grief. How could she ever have thought him heartless? Despite his unhappy childhood, and the brutal years he had spent in the Russian army, he had loved his wife and child. But losing them had been a shattering blow; it was little wonder that he had built a wall around his heart, and if Lena Tarasov was right he would never allow any woman to break through his defences.

When Ella opened her eyes the following morning she was alone, the faint indentation on the pillow the only evidence that Vadim had slept beside her. She rolled onto his side of the bed and breathed in the evocative scent of his cologne that lingered on the sheets. Last night, his decision to confide the details of his marriage to her had given her confidence that they had passed a cornerstone in their relationship. But in the clear light of day she could not escape the stark realisation that he was still in love with his dead wife.

The fact that he had opened up his heart to her must mean something, she thought wistfully as she slid out of bed and wrapped her robe around her. His ravaged expression when he had spoken of Irina and Klara was indisputable proof that, far from being the heartless playboy she had once believed, he was capable of deep emotions. But the possibility that he could ever fall in love with her seemed as remote as ever. Vadim was tied to his past—not simply by the love he felt for his wife and child, but by guilt because he felt that he had not been a good husband and father.

Could he ever be persuaded to take another chance on

love? She cast her mind over the happy times they had spent together since they had come to Antibes. The closeness they had shared had not only been in her imagination, she thought, feeling a fragile flame of hope spark inside her. They had become friends as well as lovers, and in choosing to reveal the secrets of his past to her Vadim had shown that he trusted her.

She walked down the stairs and out to the terrace, her heart clenching when she saw him sitting at the breakfast table. It was important that she encouraged him to talk more about Irina and Klara, she decided. He had kept his pain locked away for far too long, but now he had lowered his barriers she wanted to help him come to terms with his past.

'Good morning, angel face.' Vadim lowered his newspaper when Ella approached, and gave her a cool smile that bore no hint of the raw emotions that had overwhelmed him the previous night. 'Did you sleep well?'

'I…yes, thank you,' she murmured, trying to hide her confusion that he was acting as if the events of last night had never taken place. His face was once more a handsome mask, his eyes concealed behind designer shades so that she had no clue to his thoughts. She dropped into a chair opposite him, and poured herself a glass of orange juice while she assembled the words she wanted to say. 'How are you feeling this morning?' She bit her lip when his dark brows winged upwards, and continued in a rush, 'I realise that last night it must have been very difficult for you to tell me about your wife and little girl, but I just want you to know that I…I'm here if you need to talk some more.'

'You mean you are offering to be…what, exactly? My counsellor?' Vadim suggested sardonically.

The faint mockery in his voice caused Ella's heart to dip, and she stared at him, searching his face desperately for some sign of the man who had opened his emotions to her the previous night.

'I'm offering my support,' she told him quietly. 'You've bottled up your grief about Irina and Klara for far too long and I want to help you.'

A nerve jumped in Vadim's cheek as he stared at Ella's beautiful face. She was so very lovely. His eyes strayed to her pale gold hair that fell in a silky curtain around her shoulders. He had never felt as close to any other human being as he did to this woman, but his every instinct was to fight the feelings she evoked in him. He did not fear any man, but emotions scared the hell out of him, he acknowledged grimly. He bitterly regretted revealing his past to her. It made him feel vulnerable and exposed, and the look of pity in her eyes made him want to weep, as if he were once again the small boy who had prayed every night that his mother would come back to him.

'I don't need your help, or your support,' he said abruptly. 'The past is gone, and no amount of talking will bring Irina and Klara back. You are my mistress, Ella—nothing more— and all I want from you is mind-blowing sex.'

Ella flinched as if he had slapped her, and she blinked hard in a desperate attempt to dispel the tears that blurred her vision. Vadim could not have made it plainer that she meant nothing more to him than a convenient sex partner. She had entered into an affair with him confident that her emotions would not get involved, but, fool that she was, she had repeated the mistake her mother had made and fallen in love with a man who did not love her. Unlike her father, who had been incapable of love, Vadim had proved that his emotions ran deep, but his heart belonged to his dead wife.

The sheer hopelessness of loving him swept over her; and with it a feeling of nausea that made her jump to her feet, terrified that she was actually going to be sick in front of him. She had felt queasy for the past few days, and had lost her appetite—classic symptoms that a migraine was brewing.

Vadim was watching her through narrowed eyes. She could not bear for him to realise how much he had hurt her and she forced a brittle smile. 'Well, I'm glad you've clarified my role in your life. If you'll excuse me, I need to take a couple of headache tablets,' she said coolly, before she hurried back into the house.

Vadim walked into the bedroom an hour later and found Ella sitting on the balcony, apparently engrossed in her book. He stared intently at her pale face, and she was glad that her sunglasses hid her red-rimmed eyes.

'Something has come up,' he said abruptly. 'I have to go to Prague for an urgent business meeting. The maid has packed a case for you. I thought we'd spend a few days there and play tourist. Have you ever been to Prague?'

'I performed there once,' Ella replied slowly, 'but I didn't get a chance to look around the city.' She hesitated, feeling her heart splinter. Earlier, she had fled from Vadim in tears, and after an hour of soul-searching she had reached the conclusion that she could not continue her relationship with him knowing that, while he was the love of her life, his heart belonged to Irina.

Why not enjoy one last trip with him? whispered a voice in her head. She would love to go to Prague with him—but then she'd happily fly to the moon with him if he asked her, she acknowledged heavily. She had always known their affair couldn't last, but she hadn't envisaged that ending it would feel as though her heart was being ripped out.

'As a matter of fact I really need to go back to London. Marcus phoned yesterday evening while you were in the shower,' she explained, flushing as she uttered the lie. 'He told me that rehearsals for the film score we will be recording have been brought forward.'

Vadim's eyes narrowed on the twin spots of colour that flared briefly on her pale face before they faded again, leaving her looking like a fragile ghost. She had seemed unwell for the last few days, but had dismissed his concern, saying merely that she was tired. It was a reasonable explanation, considering that they frequently made love several times a night, he conceded. But it wouldn't hurt to insist that she see a doctor.

'Why didn't you mention your conversation with Marcus last night?' he queried.

'I…I forgot.' Ella dropped her eyes from his. 'Give me ten minutes to pack and I'll catch a lift to the airport with you. I'm sure I'll be able to book a last-minute flight home.'

'I told you—the maid has packed a case for you.'

The edge of impatience in Vadim's voice exacerbated Ella's tension, but she forced herself to meet his gaze. 'I need to pack my own clothes, that I brought with me.' She paused and then said quietly, 'I've been in touch with Uncle Rex. He's found a flat big enough for me to keep my piano, and I intend to move out of Kingfisher House as soon as I get back to London.'

Vadim regarded her silently for long, tense moments which stretched her nerves to snapping point. 'This is all very sudden,' he drawled. 'What has triggered this unexpected urgency to return to London, Ella?'

'I've been thinking about it for a few days,' she mumbled untruthfully.

'Really? So every time we made love recently you were plotting to leave me?' he queried coldly.

'It's time we moved on,' Ella said desperately, when anger blazed in Vadim's eyes. 'Our affair was only ever a temporary arrangement, to last as long as either of us wanted it to.' She reminded him of his words when they had first become lovers.

Vadim could feel his heart slamming against his ribs. Sure, he remembered what he had said when he'd laid down the rules of their relationship, but he had never expected that he would want to change those rules—and he'd certainly never contemplated that Ella would be the one to call time on their affair.

'You know as well as I do that this isn't over,' he said harshly. He pulled her to her feet and wrenched the edges of her robe apart, ignoring her startled cry as he stared down at her naked body. 'Do you want me to prove it to you?' he demanded, moving his hand to his belt. 'I could make love to you right now, Ella, and you wouldn't stop me.'

'No!' The flash of fear in her eyes stopped him in his tracks, and he flung her from him, frustration boiling up inside him.

'Why?' he bit out, nostrils flaring as he sought to control his temper and suppress the fear churning in his stomach. He didn't want to lose her. Hell—where had that thought come from? he asked himself as he raked a hand through his hair.

'Being here with you has been…fun,' she told him, praying he would not hear the tremor in her voice. 'But music is my life, and I need to focus exclusively on my playing to succeed in my career. I don't have time for distractions. I thought you would understand,' she said tremulously when his jaw tightened. 'You admitted that you felt the same drive and determination when you were building your company.'

It was the truth, but he did not like having the tables turned on him, Vadim thought grimly. Ella had a fantastic career ahead of her, and to achieve the success she deserved she *would* need to dedicate herself utterly to her music. He had no right to try and interfere with the life she had mapped out. But the thought of letting her go tore at his insides. These past weeks at the villa had been the happiest of his life, and he was shocked to realise how much he had enjoyed the time away from his work schedule. He had finally mastered the art of delegation, and had handed tasks over to his chief executives so that he could spend more time with Ella. It was bitterly ironic that she was citing the demands of her career as the reason why she wanted to end their relationship.

But if she thought he would beg her to stay with him she could think again. They'd had a good time, but she was right: it was time to move on. It was not as though their affair could ever have been more than a brief fling. He had proved that he was no good at relationships, and he had no intention of going down that road again.

He swung back to face her, and felt a hand squeeze his heart when he saw the glimmer of tears in her eyes. She was so very lovely, but she clearly had her own agenda—and beautiful blondes were ten a penny for a playboy billionaire. 'If that's really what you want, you'd better pack whatever you want to take with you,' he said coolly, forcing himself to turn and walk away from her. 'I'll meet you downstairs in fifteen minutes. Do you want me to phone the airport and see if I can book you a flight to London?'

'Please.' Somehow Ella managed to articulate the word, but the minute he walked out of the bedroom she raced into the bathroom and was violently sick.

It was over. And, from his faintly bored attitude, Vadim clearly did not give a damn. Those times when he had made love to her with tenderness as well as passion, whispering words to her in Russian as he cradled her in his arms, had meant nothing to him, and she had been a fool to hope that he was beginning to care for her.

Somehow she dragged herself back into the bedroom, dressed quickly in the clothes she had brought with her from Paris and packed her few belongings. Her violin was in its case next to the bed, and she picked it up and hurried out of the room, tears burning the back of her throat when she glanced back at the bed where every night Vadim had taken her to that magical place she had believed was uniquely theirs.

Doubtless he would soon replace her with another mistress, she thought bleakly. Images of him making love to another woman lacerated her heart, and she flew down the stairs and across the hall to the front door of the villa.

He was lowering the roof of the Aston Martin while talking on his mobile phone. Maybe he was arranging her flight home? Misery swept through her as she faced the devastating reality that he would never hold her in his arms again. She felt dizzy with grief, and as she walked down the front steps she lost her footing. Her startled cry rent the air, and she heard Vadim swear violently, saw him move towards her—and then there was nothing.

She came round to find that Vadim had laid her on the back seat of his car. She lifted her lashes and stared groggily at him, shocked by how grey he looked beneath his tan. His jaw was rigid, and for a moment something blazed in his eyes, before he moved away from her and leapt into the driver's seat.

'My violin!' she cried, staring back at her violin and her suitcase, lying on the driveway as the car sped away. 'Vadim, I can't go to the airport without it.'

'We're not going to the airport,' he informed her tersely. 'I'm taking you to the local hospital.'

'The hosp…? I fainted, that's all.' She sat up, and the wind whipped her hair across her face.

'Women do not faint without a reason,' he said grimly. 'You're as pale as death, you've barely eaten a thing all week, and you collapsed and would have fallen down a set of stone steps if I hadn't caught you. I have a friend who is a doctor. Claude will check you out, and if he says you're well enough to travel, then I'll take you to the airport.'

His implacable tone warned Ella that arguing would be futile. How could she tell him that she had suffered an extreme physical reaction to the mental anguish she felt at the ending of their affair? He would guess that she was in love with him, and then her pride as well as her heart would be in tatters.

At the hospital they were met by a nurse, who whisked Ella off to check her blood pressure and requested a urine sample before ushering her into the doctor's office.

Claude Arnot stood up from his desk and indicated that she should take a seat. She glared at Vadim when he dropped into the chair next to her, but his hard smile told her that he was staying for her consultation with the doctor.

'Vadim tells me you have lost your appetite recently, Mademoiselle Stafford. Do know why that could be?'

She shrugged. 'I've been feeling a bit nauseous, but I suffer from occasional migraines, and I suspect I'm going to be hit by one any day soon.'

The doctor nodded. 'Is everything else normal? Your periods, for instance? When was the date of your last one?'

'I don't really know.' Ella frowned, trying to remember, and feeling ridiculously embarrassed at discussing something so personal in front of Vadim. 'They've never been regular. In fact my GP told me it's possible that I will need fertility treatment if I ever want children. But the demands of my career mean that I will probably never choose to have a family,' she explained, with a faint catch in her voice.

They were interrupted by the arrival of the nurse, who handed the doctor some notes. He skimmed through them in silence. He would probably say that she was anaemic, Ella decided. She had forgotten to mention that her GP had prescribed a course of iron pills last year, when a blood test had shown that she was suffering from an iron deficiency. She wished he would hurry up. Sitting next to Vadim, breathing in the familiar sandalwood scent of his cologne, was torture, and she was in danger of flinging herself at him and begging him to take her to Prague with him.

She gave a start when Claude Arnot cleared his throat, and looked across the desk at him, puzzled by his sympathetic smile.

'I hope your career is not *too* demanding, Mademoiselle Stafford,' the doctor said gently, 'because you are pregnant.'

CHAPTER ELEVEN

AFTERWARDS, Ella had no clear recollection of walking out of the consulting room. On the periphery of her shell-shocked mind she heard Vadim's terse voice, asking if the test indicated when she might have conceived, and heard the doctor's reply that she was about six weeks into her pregnancy.

It must have happened at Kingfisher House, right at the beginning of their affair, she thought dazedly, as Vadim gripped her elbow and whisked her back to the car. His thoughts were obviously on the same track, and as he fired the engine he said harshly, 'That first time in the summerhouse, during the storm—I didn't use protection. I assumed, since you did not say anything, that there had been no repercussions after my carelessness, but clearly that is not the case.'

He was white-lipped with shock, and Ella sank back in her seat as they sped back to the villa, trembling with reaction to the astounding news that she was carrying Vadim's baby. The possibility had not crossed her mind. As she had explained to Dr Arnot, her periods had never been regular, but she had not bothered to seek a reason because she had assumed that, as she never planned to get married, she would never have children.

From the look of fury on Vadim's face it was clear he did not welcome the news that she was expecting his child. A wave of protectiveness flooded through her, so strong that she placed her hands on her flat stomach. Poor baby! At this early stage it was technically only a cluster of cells, but to Ella it was a child that she and Vadim had created. Could their baby possibly know that it was unwelcome? The idea was so unbearable that tears filled her eyes, and love swept through her with the force of a tidal wave; love for the baby she had never expected to conceive, but who already aroused such a fierce maternal instinct within her that she knew she would give her life for her child.

But what was she going to do? How would she manage as a single mother? She could not realistically pursue a career as a soloist when it would mean dragging a young child around the world each time she toured, she acknowledged heavily. Lost in her thoughts, she did not notice that they had driven through the gates of the Villa Corraline until Vadim cut the engine, and her heart thudded frantically in her chest when he led the way into the house in a grim silence that shredded her nerves.

He had no right to be so angry, she thought rebelliously when he ushered her into the sitting room and followed her inside, closing the door with an ominous thud. He had admitted that her pregnancy was due to *his* mistake. He was probably furious because he believed she would demand a huge maintenance agreement for their child—but he had no need to worry, she thought fiercely. She wanted nothing from him. Somehow she would manage to bring up her child alone.

Vadim crossed to the bar and poured himself a large vodka, uncaring that it was only eleven a.m. His hand shook as he lifted the glass to his lips, and he gulped the clear liquid down in one, feeling the alcohol warm the blood that had frozen in his veins. Ella had moved to stand by the window and sunlight danced over her hair, turning it into a river of gold that flowed down her back. She was so beautiful—but he could not bear to look at her, and he gripped the glass in his hand so tightly that it was in danger of shattering.

'No wonder you were so desperate to leave France and go back to London,' he bit out savagely. 'I assume you weren't going to tell me you are carrying my child.'

Startled by the accusation, Ella shook her head. 'I had no idea I was pregnant,' she defended herself.

'How could you not have known?' Vadim demanded blisteringly. 'You *must* have known, and that's why, out of the blue, you announced that you wanted to end our affair—because you didn't want me to find out.' He drew a ragged breath and fought to control the emotions that had been building inside him since the shocking revelation that Ella had conceived his baby.

'*Push me higher on the swing, Papa...*' Klara's sweet voice echoed in his mind, and for a moment he saw her face with such crystal clarity that he felt he could almost reach out and touch her, hold her wriggling little body in his arms and tell her she was his princess. Grief pierced him like an arrow through the heart. Klara had gone, and he would never hear her laughter again. But now, amazingly, there would be another child—not a replacement for the child he had lost, but a precious gift he would treasure, a second chance at fatherhood that he would not fail.

He stared at Ella, recalling the several occasions when she had stated that she did not plan to have children because she wanted to concentrate on her career, and a sickening suspicion crept into his mind. 'Do you intend to go ahead with the pregnancy?' he demanded coldly. 'Or was the reason for your sudden decision to rush back to England so that you could have a termination?' He ignored her shocked gasp and continued harshly, '*You* might not want this baby, but I do. I realise that nine months of pregnancy will interrupt your career, but I will compensate you financially, and from the moment the baby is born I will take charge of it. You will be able to have your life back.'

Ella opened her mouth, but her vocal cords had been strangled and no sound emerged. 'You're offering to…to *buy* the baby from me?' she faltered at last, shock swiftly replaced by searing rage. 'How dare you make the appalling suggestion that I would even *think* about ending my pregnancy?' Her emotions were on a rollercoaster, and her anger died as quickly as it had come as hurt unfurled inside her. How could she ever have believed that she and Vadim were growing close when he could think that of her? It proved that he did not know her at all, she thought miserably.

But in truth his reaction to the news of her pregnancy had taken her by surprise. She had not expected him to want this baby. But she had seen the pain in his eyes when he had told her about the tragic loss of his daughter—she should have known that he would feel protective of the child she was carrying.

'I might not have planned to have children, but I want this baby, and I will love it and be the best mother I possibly can,' she said shakily. 'If you want to be involved in our child's upbringing, then I'm sure we can work out arrangements for shared access and…and visiting rights,' she pushed on, her voice wavering slightly when Vadim's brows drew together in a thunderous frown.

'I have no intention of *visiting* my child,' he grated. 'I want to be a proper, hands-on father.' The kind of father he should have been to Klara, instead of spending long hours at his office.

'But…what will we do?' Ella queried uncertainly, wondering if Vadim would demand that their baby should spend a few weeks, or even months, living with each of them in turn. An arrangement along those lines might enable her to continue with her career, she acknowledged. But she knew instantly that she would not be able to bear being parted from her child for even a day, and compared to being a mother her career was no longer the most important thing in her life.

'I'm not sure how we'll sort out the details,' Vadim admitted. 'All I know is that I am determined to take an active role in my child's upbringing. Maybe we could continue with the arrangement to share Kingfisher House, so that the baby lives with both of us?'

Ella frowned, wondering if he meant that she and the baby would live in the caretaker flat, enabling him to see his child regularly while he maintained his bachelor lifestyle in the main part of the house. He had made it clear that he wanted his baby, but had made no mention of how he saw *her* future role in his life. He might bring other women back for the night, she thought, blanching at the idea of living next door to him, knowing that he was making love to a new mistress in the master bedroom where he had once made love to her.

'That would be unbearable!' she burst out, feeling sick with misery. 'I want to live in my own house and lead my own life.'

Did the new life she suddenly seemed so keen on include dating other men? Vadim wondered furiously. He felt as though he had been kicked in the gut by her adamant refusal to share Kingfisher House with him. It seemed the obvious solution, which would enable them to both care for the baby, but Ella had sounded horrified by the suggestion.

What if she had a relationship with some guy and invited him to stay the night—or even move in with her? Jealousy burned like acid in his stomach as he imagined another man making love to her, and perhaps acting as a father figure to his child. The prospect was intolerable, and his resolve hardened.

'I should warn you that if we cannot reach an amicable

agreement on shared care then I will fight for sole custody of our child—and I will win,' he said harshly.

Ella paled. He was deadly serious, she realised shakily. She had always known that beneath his charisma there was a ruthless side to him, and here now was proof of his lethal power. 'You wouldn't…' she said shakily.

'I can afford the best lawyers; and I can give our child a stable home, an excellent education—everything that money can buy,' he listed harshly. 'Whereas you…' He raked his eyes over her slender figure. 'You have admitted that you need to practise your violin for five or six hours a day, and playing with an orchestra means that you would be at work in the evenings. What do you propose to do with our child then? Leave him or her in the care of a babysitter? And what about when you are on tour—will you drag the baby around Europe with you?'

'I don't know!' she cried, hating him for voicing exactly the same problems she had foreseen. 'Despite what you think, finding out that I'm pregnant was a complete shock, and right now my world feels as though it has been turned upside down,' she admitted huskily, brushing her hand across her eyes to wipe away her tears.

The betraying gesture tugged on Vadim's conscience and his anger drained away—to be replaced with a strong urge to haul her into his arms and simply hold her, tell her that he would take care of her and their baby. But she had made it clear that she did not want his care. Pain lanced him, and he moved away from her, needing to put some space between them while he brought his emotions back under control. He who prided himself on having dismissed emotions from his life! That was a laugh, he thought savagely. Ella had got him so stirred up that he couldn't think straight, and his normal cool logic had been replaced with a seething mass of emotions.

Ella was right. The news of her pregnancy had been a shock for both of them, and if she felt anything like him then she was beyond rational thought right now. They needed a breathing space, and whatever else was happening in his life the logical part of his brain reminded him that he still needed to go to Prague. His dedication to his business was still total, and iron self-discipline won over the urge to send one of his executives to the meeting so that he could remain at the villa with Ella.

'We'll continue with this discussion in a couple of days, when I get back from my trip,' he told her brusquely, silently acknowledging that there was nothing to discuss. He had not expected to be a father again, but Ella had conceived his baby, and he was utterly determined to bring his child up and be the best father he could.

'You need to sit down before you fall down,' he growled, concern flooding through him when she swayed on her feet. She looked like a wraith; all wide, bruised eyes in a face the colour of parchment, and with a muttered oath he lifted her into his arms and strode out of the room and up the stairs. 'I'll tell Hortense to bring you something to eat,' he told her, referring to the good-natured housekeeper and cook who worked at the villa. 'Rest for a while—for the baby's sake,' he reminded her when she opened her mouth to argue, and took advantage of her parted lips to bestow a brief, stinging kiss that drew Ella's instant response and left her full of despair as she watched him stride out of the room, the taste of him lingering on her skin.

Minutes later she heard the Aston Martin roar down the drive. The dramatic events of the morning had left her physically and emotionally drained, and she lay lethargically on the bed, feeling too weak to move.

She was still stunned that she was going to have a baby. It was unexpected and unplanned, but as the news sank in she felt a piercing joy at the prospect of being a mother. Her mind turned to Vadim's threat that he would fight for custody of the baby, and her happiness dissolved. She sat up and instinctively placed her hand on her stomach, as if to protect the tiny speck of life within her.

As Vadim had pointed out, he could afford to hire the best lawyers, and there was a strong possibility he would win a court battle. Panic swept through her, destroying all rational thought. She would never hand over her child—never. All she could think of was to leave the villa before he got back from Prague and flee back to England. She would move out of Kingfisher House and go away somewhere, cover her tracks so that he could not find her, she decided frantically. And, filled with a sudden energy born of desperation, she jumped up, grabbed her violin and the suitcase that the maid must have rescued from the driveway after Vadim had driven her to the hospital, and raced down the stairs.

Vadim strode through the hotel lobby, trying to focus his mind on the take-over bid of a media company that he was about to clinch. The deal was an important one, hence his decision to personally attend the meeting to hammer out the last remaining details. But instead of profit margins all he could think about was Ella.

Ella and his baby. Thoughts of his unborn child eased the ache in his heart caused by the death of his little daughter so many years ago. He had mourned his wife too, but his grief at losing Irina had been mingled with a feeling of guilt that he had not loved her as deeply as she had loved him. He had cared for her, and had tried to do his best for her, but he had not felt the earth-shattering, volcanic eruption of emotion that the poets described as love.

In all honesty he had not believed that such a powerful love even existed, and if it did he had always been certain that he was not capable of it. But now, as he stood on the steps of the hotel and stared across the ancient city of Prague, he realised that his life was a series of dull black and white images without Ella.

If she had been with him they would have explored Prague together. She loved history, and would have been fascinated by the castle, and the beautiful Basilica of St George. Maybe they would have taken a boat trip down the River Vltava, and then eaten in one of the charming little restaurants in the Old Town before returning to their hotel to make love with a passion that touched his soul.

He missed her, he acknowledged, feeling the ache in his chest grow and expand until it seemed to encompass his whole body. He wanted to be with her. The thought drummed through his veins, and suddenly it seemed as if a curtain had lifted in his mind and he saw what a blind fool he had been.

During the weeks they had spent together in Antibes he had refused to admit that he was falling in love with her. He had been afraid of the emotions she stirred in him, and determined to fight his feelings. But now it hit him that what he really had to fear was a life without Ella. His heart was beating too fast, and his skin felt clammy as the emotions he had tried so hard to deny surged through him with the unstoppable force of a tidal wave. Prague looked beautiful in the sunshine, but he turned his back on the city and strode back into the hotel, to inform the receptionist that he was curtailing his visit.

In the taxi to the airport he phoned his PA and asked her to postpone the meeting, and then he called his chief executive and ordered him to catch the next flight to Prague. The delay meant there was a danger they would lose the deal, but for the first time in his life he had something he cared about more than business—his one thought was to get back to the Villa Corraline as quickly as possible.

He should not have left Ella alone. Especially when she was in a state of shock after finding out that she was pregnant. He believed now that she had not known she was expecting his baby. Unlike many women he had met she was not a clever actress, and the expression of stunned disbelief on her face when the doctor had given her the news had been real. He could not believe he had made that crass accusation that she had planned to get rid of the baby. The Ella he had come to know was simply not capable of such an action. But, having accepted that fact, he also had to accept that she had announced she was going back to London because she wanted to end their relationship.

Guilt clawed in his gut when he recalled their last explosive confrontation. They both wanted their child, but instead of having a rational discussion about how best they could bring up the baby he had threatened her with a custody battle. No wonder he had glimpsed real fear in her eyes. In her mind he must seem as much of a bully as her father had been—that same father who, when she was a child, had locked her in the tower room of the family mansion, knowing that she was terrified the place was haunted.

He could not blame her if she refused to have anything more to do with him, he thought bleakly, cursing the traffic that clogged the roads leading to the airport. He could only pray that she would give him another chance and allow him to explain just what she meant to him.

Silver moonlight danced across the waves which gently lapped the shore. The beach was silent, the air warm and still, and the fine white sand felt soft beneath Ella's feet as she strolled along by the water's edge.

For the first time since she had learned that she was pregnant with Vadim's baby a sense of calm had settled over her, and she knew that her decision to remain in France and wait for him had been the right one. She had been in the taxi, on the way to the airport, when she had come to her senses and accepted that running away was not the answer. She couldn't live as a fugitive for the rest of her life, and, more importantly, she accepted that she could not deny Vadim his child.

Back at the villa she had tried to remain calm, and for the baby's sake had forced herself to eat something. But tonight sleep had proved impossible, and after tossing restlessly in the big lonely bed for over an hour she had finally got up, slipped on her grey silk robe and walked down to the beach.

She missed Vadim, she acknowledged as she stared up at the crescent moon and the stars that studded the sky like diamonds on a velvet backdrop. Apart from the few days when she had been in Paris, this was the first night they had spent apart since they had become lovers. It was such a short time, really, yet her life seemed to have been entwined with his for ever, and she could not imagine living without him.

Now that she was over the shock of discovering that she was pregnant, she was able to think rationally again. Vadim's threat to fight for custody of their child was understandable when she knew that he still grieved for the daughter he had lost. But she was certain he would never force her to hand over her baby.

It all came down to trust, she mused as she turned to walk back towards the house. Her father had been a cruel man, who had delighted in hurting her and her mother, but Vadim was nothing like him. She could not deny him his chance to be a father again, and when he returned from Prague she would tell him that she accepted his proposal to share Kingfisher House, so that they could bring up the baby together. It would not be easy, living close to him yet being shut out of his life. But she loved him so much that she was prepared to sacrifice her happiness for his.

Lost in her thoughts, she gave a start when she heard her name being called across the dark beach. Vadim was calling her. But Vadim was in Prague. She gave herself a mental shake, convinced that she had imagined his voice. Loving him was turning her into a madwoman, she thought ruefully.

'*Ella…*'

A figure came running out of the shadows, tearing across the sand towards her. 'Vadim?' Even from a distance she sensed his urgency, and without thinking of anything but her need to be with him she began to run too.

He reached her and swept her into his arms, crushing her against his chest so that the breath was driven from her body. The expression on his face was tortured, his brilliant blue eyes blazing with an emotion that made her heart miss a beat. She could not imagine why he was there, and she stared up at him in confusion when she felt a shudder run through his big body. What could have happened to cause him to look so *shattered*?

'I thought you had gone—that I had driven you away…' His voice was muffled against her throat, and her heart turned over when she felt wetness against her skin.

'Why are you here?' she asked shakily. 'Why aren't you in Prague, finalising your deal?'

'I suddenly realised what was truly important to me.' His Russian accent was very pronounced, his voice as deep and haunting as the notes of a cello. 'I thought I had terrified the life out of you with my unforgivable threat to fight you for custody of the baby. I was sure you had decided to leave me, and when I arrived at the villa and saw your violin was missing I knew I had been the biggest fool on the planet.'

The expression blazing in his eyes made Ella tremble, but she was afraid that her mind was playing tricks, seeing what it wanted to see. 'I had planned to leave,' she admitted, 'but halfway to Nice I realised that I couldn't go. Our baby needs both its parents,' she said huskily.

Vadim closed his eyes briefly and sent up a silent prayer. His heart was slamming beneath his ribs as he tightened his arms around Ella and pressed his lips to her brow, utterly undone by the emotions storming through him. 'When I walked into the empty house I was afraid that I had left it too late to tell you—' He broke off, his throat convulsing, and Ella stroked a trembling hand over his face.

'Tell me what?' she whispered.

Her hair smelled of lemons. He would carry the evocative scent to his grave—a tangible reminder of the woman who had stolen his heart. Taking a deep breath, he stared down into her smoke-soft eyes. 'That I love you,' he said unsteadily. 'With all my heart and everything I am, *angel moy*.' He gave a faint smile at her stunned expression. 'You are my world, Ella, and I am nothing without you.'

'Vadim...' Tears blurred her eyes and she placed a trembling finger across his lips, no thought in her head to hold back the words she had wanted to say for so long. 'I love you too— desperately—and I will do so for ever,' she added fiercely, realising from his stunned expression that he needed convincing of the depth of her love for him.

'Then why did you say that living at Kingfisher House with me would be unbearable?' he demanded raggedly.

She blushed. 'Because I knew that I loved you, and I couldn't stand the thought of sharing the house but not your life.'

'I only said I would fight you for the baby because I hated the idea of you living away from me and having other relationships,' Vadim admitted, tangling his fingers in her long blonde hair and tipping her face to his. 'I refused to admit how much you meant to me until I went to Prague and it finally hit me how goddamned miserable I was without you.'

His tension suddenly eased, and he stared down at her, his blue eyes blazing with such tenderness, such love, that tears blurred Ella's vision.

'I want to spend the rest of my life with you, Ella,' he said softly. 'Will you marry me, my angel?'

He felt her tremble, and mistook her joy for apprehension. 'I know you have bad memories of your parents' marriage, but I would never do anything to hurt you. I intend to spend the rest of my life taking care of you, and the baby, and any other children we might have.'

Ella's heart turned over at the urgency in his voice. 'I think we'd better concentrate on one baby at a time,' she teased gently. She hesitated, and then said huskily, 'I thought you had buried your heart with Irina.'

Vadim shook his head. 'I loved her, but I'm ashamed to say that I took her for granted. I was ambitious, and often I was so busy chasing deals that I put her second to my business. When I met you, you dominated my thoughts from the start— and I knew I was in trouble when I realised I would rather spend time with you than at work. I thought I could have an affair with you and then dismiss you from my life, but deep down I think I always recognised that you are the other half of my soul, *angel moy*, and I will love you until I die.'

He cupped her chin and lowered his mouth to hers, claiming her lips in an evocative kiss that made her feel as though fireworks were exploding inside her. 'I was determined not to fall in love with you,' she whispered. 'But I couldn't resist you. And eventually I was forced to admit that I didn't want to run from you, but to you. You are my life, my love…'

'My wife?' he queried gently.

'Yes.' Another tear trickled down her face and he caught it

with his mouth, so that she tasted the salt on his lips when he kissed her again, this time with a sensual passion that sent fire coursing through her veins. He was the love of her life, and she told him so when he parted her silvery robe and it whispered to the ground. She stood before him, pale and ethereal in the moonlight. She told him again when he kissed her mouth and throat and breasts, catching her breath when he caressed each dusky nipple with his tongue before he knelt to press hungry kisses over her flat stomach, where their baby lay, and down to the cluster of gold curls between her thighs.

The sensation of his wickedly inventive tongue probing her slick wetness made her cry out, and she curled her fingers into his thick black hair as the intimate caress sent her close to the edge. He stripped out of his clothes with an uncharacteristic lack of grace that made her love him more, and then he spread her on the sand and moved over her, his brilliant blue eyes locked with hers as he entered her and made them one.

'I thought it was just good sex,' she said shyly, her eyes widening until they reflected the silvery gleam of the moon as he set a rhythm that drove them both higher.

'It was *never* just sex with you, angel,' he groaned, feeling the first delicious spasms of her orgasm close around him. 'Every time I made love to you it was with my heart as well as my body—I just didn't want to admit that you had such a hold on me.'

He moved inside her, and suddenly there was no need for words when their bodies could express the deep and abiding love they felt for each other. It was a love that would last a lifetime and beyond, Vadim vowed, and was finally able to translate the Russian words he had whispered to her every time they had made love, so that she was in no doubt as to how much she meant to him.

EPILOGUE

THEY were married a month later, in a simple but moving ceremony in the grounds of the Villa Corraline. Vadim's close friend Sergey Tarasov acted as best man, and Jenny flew over to be Ella's maid of honour. At the reception, Lena Tarasov commented that she had always suspected Vadim had fallen for Ella like a ton of bricks, and the love that blazed in Vadim's eyes when he looked at his new wife supported her theory.

They returned to London so that Ella could continue to play with the RLO, but, much to Marcus Benning's disappointment, she announced that she no longer intended to pursue a solo career now that she was going to be a mother.

Their baby daughter was born the following spring, when the cherry blossom trees in the garden at Kingfisher House were in full bloom. They named her Odette, because in the womb she had kicked hardest every time Ella played Tchaikovsky's score from *Swan Lake*, and from birth she was instantly pacified by the sound of the violin.

'Perhaps she'll grow up to be a famous virtuoso,' Ella mused one evening as Vadim cradled his newborn daughter, who was refusing to go to sleep and squawked a protest every time her mother put down her bow. 'Although, of course, she might be a genius business tycoon like her father.'

'Whatever she chooses to do in the future, she will always know that she is loved,' Vadim replied deeply. 'Just as I hope her mother knows that she is the love of my life.'

He lifted his head and trapped her gaze, the tenderness and love in his brilliant blue eyes filling Ella with joy. 'As you are mine,' she promised him fervently. 'Now and for always, my love.'

* * * * *

Harlequin offers a romance for every mood!
See below for a sneak peek from our suspense romance line
Silhouette® Romantic Suspense.
Introducing HER HERO IN HIDING by
New York Times *bestselling author Rachel Lee.*

Kay Young returned to woozy consciousness to find that she was lying on a soft sofa beneath a heap of quilts near a cheerfully burning fire. When she tried to move, however, everything hurt, and she groaned.

At once she heard a sound, then a stranger with a hard, harsh face was squatting beside her. "Shh," he said softly. "You're safe here. I promise."

"I have to go," she said weakly, struggling against pain. "He'll find me. He can't find me."

"Easy, lady," he said quietly. "You're hurt. No one's going to find you here."

"He will," she said desperately, terror clutching at her insides. "He always finds me!"

"Easy," he said again. "There's a blizzard outside. No one's getting here tonight, not even the doctor. I know, because I tried."

"Doctor? I don't need a doctor! I've got to get away."

"There's nowhere to go tonight," he said levelly. "And if I thought you could stand, I'd take you to a window and show you."

But even as she tried once more to pull away the quilts, she remembered something else: this man had been gentle when he'd found her beside the road, even when she had kicked and clawed. He hadn't hurt her.

Terror receded just a bit. She looked at him and detected signs of true concern there.

The terror eased another notch and she let her head sag on the pillow. "He always finds me," she whispered.

"Not here. Not tonight. That much I can guarantee."

Will Kay's mysterious rescuer protect her
from her worst fears?
Find out in HER HERO IN HIDING
by New York Times *bestselling author Rachel Lee.*
Available June 2010,
only from Silhouette® Romantic Suspense.

HARLEQUIN® Romance®

GIRLS' Weekend in VEGAS

Four friends, four dream weddings!

On a girly weekend in Las Vegas, best friends Alex, Molly, Serena and Jayne are supposed to just have fun and forget men, but they end up meeting their perfect matches! Will the love they find in Vegas stay in Vegas?

Find out in this sassy, fun and wildly romantic miniseries all about love and friendship!

═══════════════════════

Saving Cinderella! by MYRNA MACKENZIE
Available June

Vegas Pregnancy Surprise by SHIRLEY JUMP
Available July

Inconveniently Wed! by JACKIE BRAUN
Available August

Wedding Date with the Best Man
by MELISSA MCCLONE
Available September

═══════════════════════

LARGER-PRINT BOOKS!

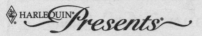

GET 2 FREE LARGER-PRINT NOVELS PLUS 2 FREE GIFTS!

YES! Please send me 2 FREE LARGER-PRINT Harlequin Presents® novels and my 2 FREE gifts (gifts are worth about $10). After receiving them, if I don't wish to receive any more books, I can return the shipping statement marked "cancel". If I don't cancel, I will receive 6 brand-new novels every month and be billed just $4.55 per book in the U.S. or $5.24 per book in Canada. That's a saving of at least 13% off the cover price! It's quite a bargain! Shipping and handling is just 50¢ per book.* I understand that accepting the 2 free books and gifts places me under no obligation to buy anything. I can always return a shipment and cancel at any time. Even if I never buy another book, the two free books and gifts are mine to keep forever.

176/376 HDN E5NG

Name	(PLEASE PRINT)	
Address		Apt. #
City	State/Prov.	Zip/Postal Code

Signature (if under 18, a parent or guardian must sign)

Mail to the **Harlequin Reader Service:**
IN U.S.A.: P.O. Box 1867, Buffalo, NY 14240-1867
IN CANADA: P.O. Box 609, Fort Erie, Ontario L2A 5X3

Not valid for current subscribers to Harlequin Presents Larger-Print books.

Are you a subscriber to Harlequin Presents books and want to receive the larger-print edition? Call 1-800-873-8635 today!

* Terms and prices subject to change without notice. Prices do not include applicable taxes. Sales tax applicable in N.Y. Canadian residents will be charged applicable provincial taxes and GST. Offer not valid in Quebec. This offer is limited to one order per household. All orders subject to approval. Credit or debit balances in a customer's account(s) may be offset by any other outstanding balance owed by or to the customer. Please allow 4 to 6 weeks for delivery. Offer available while quantities last.

Your Privacy: Harlequin Books is committed to protecting your privacy. Our Privacy Policy is available online at www.eHarlequin.com or upon request from the Reader Service. From time to time we make our lists of customers available to reputable third parties who may have a product or service of interest to you. If you would prefer we not share your name and address, please check here. ☐

Help us get it right—We strive for accurate, respectful and relevant communications. To clarify or modify your communication preferences, visit us at www.ReaderService.com/consumerschoice.

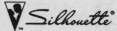

ROMANTIC

SUSPENSE

Sparked by Danger, Fueled by Passion.

NEW YORK TIMES AND *USA TODAY*
BESTSELLING AUTHOR

RACHEL LEE

BRINGS YOU AN ALL-NEW
CONARD COUNTY: THE NEXT GENERATION SAGA!

After finding the injured Kay Young on a deserted country
road Clint Ardmore learns that she is not only being hunted
by a serial killer, but is also three months pregnant.
He is determined to protect them—even if it means
forgoing the solitude that he has come to appreciate.
But will Clint grow fond of having an attractive woman
occupy his otherwise empty ranch?

Find out in

Her Hero in Hiding

Available June 2010 wherever books are sold.

Visit Silhouette Books at www.eHarlequin.com

SRS27681

Coming Next Month

in **Harlequin Presents® EXTRA.** Available May 11, 2010.

#101 THE COSTANZO BABY SECRET
Catherine Spencer
Claiming His Love-Child

#102 HER SECRET, HIS LOVE-CHILD
Tina Duncan
Claiming His Love-Child

#103 HOT BOSS, BOARDROOM MISTRESS
Natalie Anderson
Strictly Business

#104 GOOD GIRL OR GOLD-DIGGER?
Kate Hardy
Strictly Business

Coming Next Month

in **Harlequin Presents®.** Available May 25, 2010:

#2921 A NIGHT, A SECRET...A CHILD
Miranda Lee

#2922 FORBIDDEN: THE SHEIKH'S VIRGIN
Trish Morey
Dark-Hearted Desert Men

#2923 THE MASTER'S MISTRESS
Carole Mortimer

#2924 GREEK TYCOON, WAYWARD WIFE
Sabrina Philips
Self-Made Millionaires

#2925 THE PRINCE'S ROYAL CONCUBINE
Lynn Raye Harris

#2926 INNOCENT IN THE ITALIAN'S POSSESSION
Janette Kenny

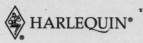

The Best Man in Texas
TANYA MICHAELS

Brooke Nichols—soon to be Brooke Baker—
hates surprises. Growing up in an unstable
environment, she's happy to be putting down
roots with her safe, steady fiancé. Then she meets
his best friend, Jake McBride, a firefighter and
former soldier who's raw, unpredictable and
passionate. With his spontaneous streak and
dangerous career, Jake is everything Brooke is
trying to avoid...so why is it so hard to resist him?

**Available June
wherever books are sold.**

"LOVE, HOME & HAPPINESS"

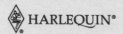
HARLEQUIN®

Showcase

On sale May 11, 2010

Reader favorites from the most talented voices in romance

Save $1.00 on the purchase of 1 or more Harlequin® Showcase books.

SAVE $1.00 on the purchase of 1 or more Harlequin® Showcase books.

Coupon expires Oct 31, 2010. Redeemable at participating retail outlets.
Limit one coupon per purchase. Valid in the U.S.A. and Canada only.

52609015

Canadian Retailers: Harlequin Enterprises Limited will pay the face value of this coupon plus 10.25¢ if submitted by customer for this product only. Any other use constitutes fraud. Coupon is nonassignable. Void if taxed, prohibited or restricted by law. Consumer must pay any government taxes. Void if copied. Nielsen Clearing House ("NCH") customers submit coupons and proof of sales to Harlequin Enterprises Limited, P.O. Box 3000, Saint John, NB E2L 4L3, Canada. Non-NCH retailer—for reimbursement submit coupons and proof of sales directly to Harlequin Enterprises Limited, Retail Marketing Department, 225 Duncan Mill Rd., Don Mills, ON M3B 3K9, Canada.

U.S. Retailers: Harlequin Enterprises Limited will pay the face value of this coupon plus 8¢ if submitted by customer for this product only. Any other use constitutes fraud. Coupon is nonassignable. Void if taxed, prohibited or restricted by law. Consumer must pay government taxes. Void if copied. For reimbursement submit coupons and proof of sales directly to Harlequin Enterprises Limited, P.O. Box 880478, El Paso, TX 88588-0478, U.S.A. Cash value 1/100 cents.

5 65373 00076 2 (8100)0 11651

® and TM are trademarks owned and used by the trademark owner and/or its licensee.
© 2009 Harlequin Enterprises Limited

HSCCOUP0410